Murder and Greed with a Hot Cup of Tea

By
Sandra Covert

Table of Contents

Prologue _____ *5*

Part 1: The Schemes of the Wicked _____ *7*

Chapter 1 _____ *8*

Chapter 2 _____ *17*

Chapter 3 _____ *21*

Chapter 4 _____ *26*

Chapter 5 _____ *40*

Chapter 6 _____ *48*

Chapter 7 _____ *54*

Part 2: The Truth Shall Set You Free _____ *65*

Chapter 8 _____ *66*

Chapter 9 _____ *69*

Chapter 10 _____ *74*

Chapter 11 _____ *84*

Chapter 12 _____ *89*

Chapter 13 _____ *102*

Chapter 14 _____ *108*

Chapter 15 _____ *120*

Chapter 16 _____ *135*

Chapter 17 _____ *148*

Chapter 18 _____ *152*

Chapter 19 _____ *157*

Chapter 20 _____ 172

Chapter 21 _____ 186

Chapter 22 _____ 199

Chapter 23 _____ 210

Chapter 24 _____ 219

Part 3: Where Does My Help Come From? _____ 226

Chapter 25 _____ 227

Chapter 26 _____ 237

Prologue

That evening, the wind was particularly heavy off the lake behind Phyllis' house. She had just retreated from her back porch to get in her kitchen's cozy, still air. It was a Saturday evening, her favorite time of day. She had formed a longtime routine of sitting on her back porch rocker when the sun started to set over the lake. But today, the wind chill drove her inside.

Her arms warmed in the sudsy water of her kitchen sink as she cleaned the last couple of dishes she had collected from the day before. Above her head was her picture window with a perfect shot of her back porch and garden area that rolled down the hill until it met her fence line.

She rinsed off the teacup she had finished earlier that evening and placed it on the drying rack. Out of sheer habit, she looked up through the window to take in the final rays of sunlight when her heart stopped in its tracks. Standing next to her garden shed was a tall, slender figure clad in black. The face was covered, and all extremities were clad in black sweaters and pants. The teacup fell from her hand and clanged against the bottom of her sink. She held her breath. The figure just stood still, staring at her.

After what felt like a small eternity, the figure shook its head slowly as if warning her about something. All Phyllis could do was stand frozen. Her hands trembled, and her heart skipped furiously.

"Jesus, help me," she whispered, afraid to move her mouth too much and initiate the figure.

Finally, the tall figure stepped back and disappeared out of view behind the garden shed. A beat later, Phyllis shook off the fright and reached for her phone on the island behind her. As her fingers trembled, she dialed her daughter's number.

"It happened again," she whispered as Agnus answered on the other end.

Part 1: The Schemes of the Wicked

"But the Lord laughs at the wicked because he sees that their day is coming." Psalm 37:13

Chapter 1

Phyllis hated the way her medicine tasted in the morning.

Maybe it was the waxy feel of it when she rested it on her tongue. Or the size of it as she swallowed with as much liquid as she could stomach.

Or maybe it was the way she felt forced to take it. Every morning, before 9:00, with a cream cheese bagel and her hot tea. She had never wanted to become a burden to those she loved as she aged. That was a promise she made over and over again in family meetings.

She'd offer, "Just put me in a home. They'll care for me, and my estate can pay for it."

Her boys listened too well. Once she started showing signs of aging, they moved far away, only to return on the occasional holiday with the new families they were building. She missed them terribly. Her oldest, George, had been the apple of her eye. Her second oldest, Thomas, was the same. But now, they were echoes of a former life, thrown across the country by the sheer mass of new responsibility and a lack of obligation. She wanted nothing more than to bring them home, but her strength had long since diminished to just a whisper, and her last ounce of fight was dimming quicker than usual.

Then there was Arlene. Phyllis was certain that if God had allowed such things, Arlene would have moved in and cared for her. Secretly, she wished this was the case. Arlene had always been the kindest of the four. She loved the Lord and had a heart for people. And as for her mother, Arlene made no secret how special her love for her was. Phyllis had always felt that the two of them were most alike. It was a fact she was proud of.

But the terrible claws of ALS had shown their selves late in Arlene's life. What started as strange weaknesses here or there and the occasional slurred word or two had recently given way to a host of issues for her mobility. She wasn't yet confined to a wheelchair, but Phyllis saw her strength wane every day. It was painful to watch.

Of course, this meant that Arlene wasn't the right choice to care for her aging mother. So, that left Agnus, her youngest daughter.

Agnus was far less compassionate by nature than her sister. Phyllis had wondered if this wasn't hereditary on her late husband's side of the gene pool. Jacob was a good man who cared for his family, but he was an old-school, heavy-handed disciplinarian who demanded respect and gave no second option. This meant harsher punishment at times than Phyllis would have preferred. And poor Agnus seemed to face the brunt of it.

Jacob made a respectable amount of money in his construction business. There was no doubt that hidden somewhere in the coffers of the family estate; there was enough to bless future generations. However, for Jacob, hard work and humility held more value than money. Perhaps this was why the family was so fortunate. For Agnus and her siblings, there was never a need left unmet. However, many wants went unfulfilled—not due to cruelty, but more so for lessons untold about working for your keep. This always bothered Agnus. As she grew older, it was obvious her parents withheld from their children. Early on, she decided to get every dollar that was due her. It became her main motivation. And she was good at it.

Her drive and determination meant that Agnus spoke her mind often. Inevitably, conflict ensued with her equally outspoken father. But Jacob had the last word every time.

Jacob had been gone for several years, and the boys were nowhere near home. So, Agnus was left unchecked—and in control by default. Phyllis was grateful, of course, for her daughter's routine check-ins and help despite having a life of her own to tend to with a child at home. Her husband, Harold, was a successful hospital administrator who brought in a large salary. On the side, he was an amateur investor who found some success in turning small sums into larger payouts. Because of this, Agnus opted to stay home and tend to her daughter. They lived an extravagant life with all the drippings of high society. Phyllis was careful never to pry into their personal, financial life. *As long as they were cared for*, that's all she prayed for. And for Agnus, that prayer was answered.

So, at 9:00 am sharp every morning, Agnus arrived to watch over Phyllis as she took her meds. Like clockwork, she brewed her tea and prepared it specially for her mother to wash down the pills. And this bright and sunny Friday morning was no different.

"Mom, why am I just now seeing a letter from Goldstein?" Agnus emerged from the hallway carrying the sealed envelope in her left hand. Her right hand cradled a maroon coffee cup from her mother's cupboard. She had been stirring the tea while she snooped in the mail basket at the front door.

Phyllis grabbed the cup and quickly downed the pills she had been delaying. The warm liquid singed her throat soothingly as they dissolved the medicine.

"I haven't checked my mail since yesterday, Agnus," she explained. "Postman must have dropped it off late yesterday evening."

Agnus was not buying it. "Mom, I told you that all legal docs must come to me and Harold. You are too unwell to bother with estate issues."

Phyllis bit her tongue. She was old, not dead. At least not yet. She had only recently started feeling "unwell" since her medication was changed. But Agnus had been convinced her cognition was waning, and she made sure everyone around her—especially Phyllis—was continuously reminded of that.

"Agnus," Phyllis said instead. "I don't know what to tell you."

Agnus rolled her eyes. "That is the problem, mom. You are quickly losing your ability to know a lot of things. Have you taken your meds this morning?"

"Yes, dear."

Phyllis reached the kitchen table and grabbed her seat and readers. All she wanted to do was read the paper for that morning. But before she could position the long-form sheet on her placemat, Agnus pulled back the seat adjacent and continued.

"I'm serious, Mom," she said with forced compassion. "It is getting worse. Just yesterday, Harold said you were muttering about intruders in the backyard."

"There were intruders, Agnus!"

Agnus quickly popped up and went to the picture window that faced Phyllis's Garden shed. The yard was spacious, with twenty blossoming plants and shrubs. Beyond a large privacy fence was a medium-sized lake.

She pointed dramatically. "How on Earth could anyone get into your backyard, Mom? You have a six-foot perimeter fence with an iron lock on both gates, and the end of the property is out to the water. There are no intruders!"

"I know what I saw," Phyllis said, her voice breaking. "I am not senile, Agnus. I am old. I saw a man in a black shirt with a hood on standing in my backyard."

"Well, Harold checked, and there were no signs of footprints, broken locks, or anything stolen. So how do you explain that?"

"I can't," Phyllis said, calming her voice. She knew the fight was pointless. If there was one thing Agnus could do better than anyone else, it was winning an argument.

"Exactly," Agnus said triumphantly. "Now, calm down before you give yourself a heart attack. I have left lunch in the fridge for today, and there's lasagna in there as well, which you can reheat for dinner. I need to run."

She tucked the unopened letter in her purse and disappeared out of the kitchen and through the front door. Agnus had become like a specter in recent weeks. She breezed in long enough to haunt Phyllis' calm mornings and then disappeared without a trace. There was no room for small talk or catching up. It was all business all the time. She seemed like she was scheming something at any given moment.

"Off to rob another person blind, I'm sure," Phyllis muttered when the coast was clear.

She did not mean it, *really*. But Phyllis knew how corrupt her daughter could be in the past. The friends she used to get what she wanted. The families her husband drove to bankruptcy with medical debt and obnoxiously high care costs. It was just last month when Cindy, Phyllis's life-long friend, received a bill for an emergency visit that cost tens of thousands of dollars. Phyllis had asked Harold to look it over, and he refused.

"Medicine isn't free, Phyllis," he answered. "If you can't afford it, then get a first aid kit."

Phyllis winced while she recalled the statement. Cindy had suffered a pulmonary embolism that could have killed her. When she got the bill, her insurance covered about 80 percent, but there were charges for care that tripled what they would cost from a drugstore. *$150 for Tylenol?* It made no sense. She was left with few options and a pile of debt. Two things that no "first aid kit" could take care of.

Phyllis shook off the memory and reached for her paper. Without warning, the room tilted on its end. Phyllis watched as the black font on the page slid at an angle toward the floor beneath her. The pictures slowly spun in their bolded ink frames, and her forehead broke out in a cold sweat.

The medicine.

Ever since she had started taking this new drug, she suffered from massive bouts of vertigo and anxiety. Her heart rate would increase on a dime, and her vision would twist and pulse for hours, leaving her completely indisposed until it passed. She would spend the entire day lying down, doing nothing until it was dark outside. When she asked her doctor about it, he shrugged it off and chalked it up to what she needed to survive.

More of Harold's cronies, she imagined.

Carefully, she followed her hallway wall with her hands and retreated to her bedroom. The shades were still down, and she cautiously felt for her bed.

It was 9:30 in the morning on a sunny Friday as Phyllis clutched her blanket in her dark room, trying her best not to float away.

Chapter 2

When the phone rang, Agnus paused before clicking the accept button on her dash.

Arlene, she muttered.

Why her sister insisted on calling her during the day made no sense to Agnus. Everyone knew how busy she was.

"Yes," she answered impolitely.

"Hey, sis," Arlene began. "Did you check on mom today?"

"Arlene, I check on mom every day."

Agnus watched as her parents' monstrous lake house shrank slowly in her rear-view mirror. The picture windows looked like they were winking at her. Conspiring with her.

"How is she doing?"

"She's pretty much the same," Agnus answered. "She is still claiming she is seeing things. I watched her take her meds and helped her with her mail. I am sure she will ball up in some corner for the rest of the day and avoid sunlight like she always does."

Agnus could hear the sigh on the other end. Her sister had always been a softy.

"It's just not like her," Arlene explained. "Mom has always loved the outdoors. I have never seen her like this."

"We need to start preparing for the inevitable, Arlene," Agnus offered. "She won't be with us much longer."

Agnus loved her mother. But her patience was thin for dealing with a lot of things, especially prolonging the inevitable. If Agnus had her way, everything would happen immediately. It just made more sense that way. Waiting around and twiddling your thumbs did nothing but delay progress. And to Agnus, progress meant security. *Money.*

Harold had exposed her early to a life full of wealth and security. Since then, she made sure her days were structured in a way that secured her future. And though she truly did love her mother, Agnus was fully aware that what would be unlocked after her death was more than enough to set her up for life and beyond.

And it all started with selling the family home.

Thankfully, with her mother's diminished state, she became more compliant with Agnus' demands. First, it was the Power of Attorney. After much prodding, she finally convinced her mother to hand over POA authority to Agnus so she could manage the estate. Of course, having Harold on her shoulder like a well-informed parrot did not hurt things either.

Immediately, she then set out to sell the home. It was a giant nest egg, rotting on a slowly eroding bank near the lake. Her mother had no business managing it, and with her increasingly alarming and erratic behavior, it was finally an easy decision. The conversation was painless, and, in the end, her mother conceded, and Agnus' girlfriend stepped in as a realtor. The commission was sure to be a big one, so Agnus figured she would share *some* of the wealth.

"It's just so odd," Arlene responded. "All of a sudden, she started to decline. Did her doctor say anything about..."

"Arlene, seriously," Agnus interrupted. "I am at every doctor's appointment. I have carried our mother across town more times than I can count. If the doctor had said something that important, don't you think I would have known? And don't you feel I would have shared it by now?"

"I know, I know," Arlene whispered defeatedly. "I am sorry, Agnus. I know you have so much stress right now. I wish I could help more. But with my condition, I just cannot..."

"It's fine, Arlene," Agnus interjected. "She is my mother, too. I have to go."

Before Arlene could say "goodbye," the phone clicked through the dash. Agnus turned her eyes back to her rearview mirror and focused on the small sign that stood out in front of her mother's home. She smiled as she mouthed the words to herself.

Sold.

Chapter 3

Phyllis could not help but feel like a spectator in her own life. The house was only on the market for seven days before Agnus informed her that it had been sold. Someone had offered $10,000 above the asking price and offered to pay in cash. This meant less time with banks and less time to emotionally prepare to leave this part of her life behind her.

Forty years. That is how long she lived in that home. It was the year after Arlene's 21st birthday. Agnus was still living at home, and her sons were gone. Jacob loved that home as much as she did. Phyllis could still see the pride on his face when they had friends over for the first time.

But now, it was gone. And with it, so many memories of a less complicated, more peaceful past.

Honestly, Phyllis was still fuzzy on the details of how she had arrived at this point. She discovered that Agnus had assumed power of attorney privilege over her assets. The news came out when she was on the phone with Goldstein, the family lawyer, during the yearly review.

"This all seems good, Phyllis," he had told her. "I'll just need to get Agnus to sign off, and then we can file it away."

"Agnus?" Phyllis asked. "Why does she need to sign anything?"

"The POA," Goldstein explained nonchalantly. "Ever since you signed it over to her, she has held signature authority on all estate decisions. She was supposed to be on this call, but there was a calendar issue, so she permitted me to have you review the report."

Permitted him? Phyllis thought. How could her youngest daughter grant permission for *anything?* It made no sense.

That next morning, when Agnus returned with her routine tea and medicine observation, she asked her what Goldstein had meant.

"You don't remember?" Agnus asked quizzically. Phyllis was not sure, but she seemed as if there was a small smile tugging at her daughter's lips.

"No," Phyllis responded quietly.

"Mom, it was last week. I brought Harold over, and we discussed you handing me POA rights to the estate. I could tell you were out of it again."

"I don't remember at all," Phyllis responded as she sipped the tea.

Oddly enough, the room started spinning right on cue. It would not be long before she was holed up again in that dark bedroom, trying to escape the panic that this vertigo threatened.

Agnus reached forward and softly touched her mother's hand. It was a rare example of compassion. Phyllis ate it up.

"Mom, don't worry about this stuff," she whispered. "I'm here to help."

Harold pulled the large SUV into the parking lot of a downtown nursing home for aging seniors. The outside of the building had faded brick with precarious vines that climbed haphazardly up the mortar. There was a bronze sign outside next to the main door. It read:

Johnson Retirement Home for Seniors.
"Come all who are weary."

Phyllis was weary. She was always tired. Maybe this was the right place after all.

After a mountain of paperwork and insurance conversations, Phyllis entered her new home on the third floor. The whole apartment was small enough to fit into her living room at the lake house. Immediately, she felt claustrophobic. The kitchen was small, but the appliances were modern. The stove was gas, which was a plus.

She found this odd. *An apartment stove that was gas-heated?* She could not imagine the cost of this place. At the back of the living room was a small sliding glass door that led to a skinny balcony. The railing was low, but the view was something else. It overlooked the city street below. For a young person, Phyllis was sure it was eye candy. But she missed her lake view. The reflection of the summer sun on the still waters. The sound of swallows in her oak trees.

Now, all that waited for her below was a busy street and hard, hot asphalt.

"Here it is, mom," said Harold. Only recently had he started calling her "mom." She found it strange. It felt forced. Like he was buttering her up.

"I like it," Phyllis squeaked. "Thank you for finding it for me."

"It's perfect for a single woman," Agnus explained as she opened cabinet doors and inspected. "Not too big. And the crew on sight will clean it for you every other day. All you have to do is relax and rest."

Great, said Phyllis sarcastically. She hated feeling so ungrateful. Agnus, in all her seriousness and harshness, meant well, she was sure. Why else would she stay so invested in caring for her mother?

"The moving truck will be here in an hour," Harold offered. "I have to head back to the hospital. We have paid the movers twenty-five hundred, so you do not have to lift a finger."

"Thank you," Phyllis responded. "I can feel my meds kicking in. I need to sit somewhere."

Agnus sprang into action. "Sit out here on the balcony, Mom."

She led Phyllis out the sliding glass door and sat her down on a small metal chair that the apartment complex provided. The fresh air was delightful on Phyllis' face, but the sunlight was torture. She held her hand over her eyes and tried to relax.

"I'll tell the movers to put your bed up first so you can go rest."

Chapter 4

The chime on Arlene's phone recentered her focus. The room was spinning again. This happened often after her morning dose. It was one of the main drawbacks of her treatment.

That and trouble breathing. Often, she wondered which was worse: ALS or the drug used to. its heavy toll.

But still, she took it not necessarily for herself but for her daughter, Allison. It was the best she could offer her. The disease was unforgiving, and soon, she would not be able to keep the worst of it at bay. But if she could squeeze out ten more years of normalcy, she would do it.

At least until she graduates college, Arlene would remind herself. Allison was a hardworking young woman who had just celebrated her 24th birthday. She was a semester and a half away from graduating college and had already mentioned her dream of starting a ministry.

Another chime on her phone. Arlene grabbed it with two hands and steadied her gaze on the notification.

Your Uber driver is 5 minutes away, it read.

She sighed a little. It was three months ago when her doctors told her it would be wise to hand in her license.

Though she was still able to drive, her vision was worsening, and her tremors were constant. It was like she was a ticking time bomb, waiting for a wrong move or involuntary tremor. At first, she fought the idea, but after the fifth broken plate at home and the third fall in public, she decided to concede. God forbid she caused a wreck.

A chilly breeze flowed freely through the busy alley street near her townhome. She adjusted herself slightly on the metal chair of her stoop. Quietly, she drifted off again and thought of her sweet daughter.

She was so proud of the woman she had become. *A prayer warrior* thought Arlene. A sense of pride swelled in her chest. She was careful not to take credit for the doings of the Lord, but she could not help but smile, knowing that her hard work had paid off in her daughter's life. She prayed earnestly for the Lord to show her how to raise a strong believer. She and her late husband made it a point each weekend to have Allison in church services. Nightly, they prayed together as a family over their meals and talked candidly about their walk with Christ at the table. Allison was inquisitive, caring, and compassionate. And now, her heart yearned to reach other young women like herself.

The cool breeze tickled the skin just above Arlene's cheek. The sound of an approaching vehicle slowly appeared from her left as her phone buzzed with the final notification, informing her that her ride had appeared.

Slowly, she pulled herself out of her chair and leaned on the wooden cane she had perched on her chair. Bit by bit, she walked down the small concrete steps and onto the sidewalk as she approached her driver. She steadied herself against the car door and slowly slid into the back seat. The door shut behind her, and the driver accelerated, heading in the direction of her mother's new home.

A twinge of restlessness played with Arlene's heart. Her last phone call with Agnus was disheartening. Arlene had noticed her mother's behavior shift since her last doctor's visit. Agnus insisted on managing her mother's affairs, which left Arlene in the dark for much of her mother's care. Typically, she would have to pry information out of her sister, and even then, it was like poking a bull.

But there was no secret that her mother was diminishing quickly. It was just odd at the timing. In Arlene's 61 years on this Earth, she never remembered a moment when her mother wasn't in her yard or sitting on her porch. Outside was her happy place. But since that last visit, she had confined herself to a dark room for hours on end. It was as if something major had switched within her like a candle had been blown out.

But what broke her heart the most was what Agnus had said happened just a week ago. Her mother had a panic attack, screaming about an intruder in her backyard. She claimed she saw a tall man dressed in black who threatened her through the window. Even after Harold had inspected for a break-in, she was convinced she was under attack.

Arlene's mother was a woman of intelligence. She was steady. But this was unlike her.

Could this really be the end? Arlene asked herself as the driver turned towards the highway and headed into town.

The thought sent chills down her spine. She was not sure how she would manage without her mother's voice in her life. And as her strength began to diminish, she found herself helpless and alone, watching her hero diminish with her.

After what seemed like an eternity, the elevator stopped at the third floor of her mother's retirement home. Thankfully, her apartment was just a few steps to the right. Arlene knocked on the door and waited for a few seconds.

With an abrupt *swish, the door swung open,* and Agnus emerged, clearly frustrated.

"Hey, Aggie," Arlene whispered.

"Hey," Agnus responded. She left the door open behind her as she turned and walked back inside.

"How's mom?" Arlene asked as she entered the main hallway. Her eyes scanned the walls. Immediately, she noticed how small the accommodations were. She was not sure how her mother would handle not being in a large home after so many years.

Agnus pointed at the back sliding glass door.

"She's out there," she answered. "See for yourself."

Arlene could see her mother's back as it pressed on the window. She was struggling. Her head was hanging forward and she cradled it in both her hands. It was like she was bracing herself to keep from falling forward.

Considering the size of the small balcony, it was wise.

"How long has she been like that?"

"It started a couple of hours ago. We have been dealing with the movers all morning. They just left. She has been catatonic since she got here."

"Is it the medication?"

"No, Arlene," Agnus sneered. "It is mom. She is getting worse. The meds are supposed to help her, but she is too far gone. I can barely get her to take them, let alone keep her lucid."

Each word stung. Arlene knew her sister was exhausted. It was a huge responsibility to take care of a sick elder, let alone watch her mother suffer. Guilt panged at Arlene's chest.

"Aggie, I am so sorry you must take on all this. I wish I could be here more."

Agnus lifted her chest slightly. "She is my mother, Arlene. It is my honor."

Arlene noticed that the word "honor" appeared forced as if Agnus had rehearsed it before. Immediately, she deleted the idea from her mind. How dare she say that of her sister? After everything?

A whistle came from the kitchen behind Agnus. Immediately she turned around and approached a tea kettle that was steaming on the stove.

Arlene thought changing the subject may do them both a favor.

"You thirsty?" she asked with a slight smile. Her sister was a coffee drinker from birth. Tea was not her forte.

"It's for mom," she answered matter-of-factly. Her back was turned as her shoulders moved in circles. Furiously, she prepared the tea as if she were conducting an orchestra.

"Ah, herbal?" Arlene asked.

Agnus sighed deeply and shook her head. "It's tea, Arlene. Just tea."

Arlene aborted the conversation. Nothing was settling the tension. Like the kettle, this air of discomfort in the cramped apartment had been brewing all day.

Agnus turned around with a freshly poured cup of tea in hand and walked to the back door where her mother was stirring. Sliding the door open, she called out.

"Mom, come inside and drink your evening tea. Arlene is here to see you."

Phyllis popped up and turned around to see her oldest daughter through the glass. When their eyes met, Arlene saw her mother smile. Right then, any idea of lunacy was erased. That was her mother; there was no denying it, and she was excited to see her.

Agnus helped her mother through the door and walked her towards the small kitchen bar where her tea sat steaming.

"Hello, love!" Phyllis called. "How are you?"

Arlene cautiously made her way to the open stool next to her mother. After a quick hug, she sat down and watched as her mother sipped the tea. Agnus stood at the other end of the bar and watched her mother drink intently, studying her.

"I am much better today, Mom. More importantly, how are you?"

Phyllis brushed her hand forward as if to wipe away the worry. "I am fine, sweetheart. Tired and old." She managed a smile and sipped her tea again.

"What do you think of your new place?" Arlene asked.

The soft light in Phyllis' eyes flickered uncertainly. After what felt like a minute, she answered diplomatically.

"I am very grateful. Your sister and brother-in-law did a wonderful job taking care of me."

Phyllis shifted her eyes towards Agnus and smiled warmly. Agnus stared intently before responding.

"It's not as large as the old home, but this way, she has the care she needs 24/7, and she's right beside the hospital."

Arlene smiled. "That is true, mama. It is good to be so close to everything you need."

Phyllis took another long sip. "I know. I just miss our home. Your father built that home with his own…"

"We know, Mom," Agnus interrupted. "We know. It was a lovely home, but it was far too large for you to tend to. This way, the money made from the home can grow in the estate, and you won't have to worry about those things any longer. You can rest and be comfortable."

Silence. Phyllis pursed her lips and placed her empty cup on the counter. Immediately, Agnus reached for it, looked inside, and put it under the faucet, cleaning it out as if it had stood there far too long.

For the next few minutes, the three women talked about the apartment, health, and family. Agnus only answered questions in quick sentences while Phyllis and Arlene talked vibrantly about their lives. Phyllis made her way down her usual list of updates, including Arlene's health, Allison's school, and how the church was carrying on. Since her recent struggle with her health, Phyllis had not been able to attend the girls' childhood church. Now, Arlene was the only connection she had to her church family.

"The service last week was wonderful," Arlene explained. "Pastor spoke on Job and made an incredible point that I had never thought of..."

Phyllis leaned sharply to her right, nearly falling out of her chair. Arlene instinctively grabbed her shoulder and tried to steady her as Agnus ran around the counter and helped pick her back up on the chair.

"Mom," Arlene nearly yelled. "Mom! Are you okay?"

Phyllis gurgled slightly, slurring her words together in a long string of incoherent babble. Agnus helped her mother to her feet and put a knowing hand on Arlene's shoulder.

"It's okay, Arlene," she stated. "This happens. It has gotten worse over the past week."

"What's happening?" Arlene yelled as she gripped the rest of her stool with her hand.

"We are not sure exactly, but it happens most evenings around this same time. It is like mom just loses it. I will get her to her bed, and she will rest. She will get past it and be okay by the morning."

Arlene's mind swirled. *Weeks?* How could her mother have been having these episodes for weeks? What was going on?

Moments later, Agnus emerged from her mother's bedroom and reentered the kitchen. She could see the worry on Arlene's face.

"I know, Arlene," she whispered. "I did not tell you this because I didn't want you to worry. Her doctor is aware. They have run tests, and we are awaiting the results. Honestly, we are not sure what is happening, but her doctors fear that her mind is...diminishing."

"'Diminishing'? What does that mean?"

"She's dying, Arlene," Agnus stated clearly. "She is dying quickly. We cannot stop it."

Tears welled up in Arlene's eyes. Her vision became blurry. *Time is running out*, she thought to herself. *Time is running out for everyone.*

Who will die first?

A few hours later, Agnus eventually left for the evening. Arlene had hailed an Uber on her phone, and the nearest driver was more than 15 minutes away. This gave her just a few more moments to see her mother before she headed out.

Softly, she made her way over to her mother's door and cracked it open. There was nothing but silence inside.

"Mama," she whispered. "I am leaving. I will give you a call in the morning."

To her surprise, her mother responded. "Arlene?"

"Hey, mama."

"Arlene, come here, love," she whispered. Arlene made her way to her mother's bedside and sat gingerly on the bed.

Her mother pointed to the lamp on the bedpost and motioned for the light to turn on. Arlene obliged.

With her face lit, Arlene had to fight off tears. Her mother looked broken and stressed. The life in her eyes was fighting to survive.

"Arlene, I need you to grab my pocketbook over on the wall," Phyllis said as she pointed to the floor. Just beside the nightstand was a black purse. Inside it, Arlene found a small envelope with her name on it.

"Grab that, dear," Phyllis said. "It's yours."

With the envelope in her hand, she began to fumble with the adhesive on the lip.

"No," Phyllis said softly as she grabbed her daughter's hand. "Not here. Open it when you are home."

Arlene nodded. "Mama, are you okay?"

Phyllis looked up at the ceiling for a moment. After a quick pause, she turned back to her daughter with a worried look.

"Arlene, something is wrong. I can feel it. What I am going through is not supposed to happen. I do not know how to explain it, but I feel like someone is after me."

Arlene gripped her mother's shaking hand tightly.

"Mama, Harold checked your backyard. There was nothing..."

Phyllis shook her head. "No, dear. Listen to me. I do not think this is just anyone. I feel like..."

She searched her daughter's eyes.

"I feel like...someone is after me. Someone I know."

"Who?" asked Arlene, utterly shaken to her core. "In all her years, she never saw her mother act this way.

"I don't know," Phyllis answered. "But I am not crazy, Arlene. I am not!"

Arlene sat back and stared. "I know, mama," she answered quickly. "Shh, mama, you need to rest."

She pushed the matted hair out of her mother's eyes and reached back for the lamp. Turning it off, she tucked her mother in just like she once was tucked in as a child.

"You're not crazy, mama," Arlene whispered. "You are tired. Just rest."

The room was silent again. She heard the soft breathing of her sleeping mother.

Her cell phone buzzed in her pocket with the notification of her approaching driver.

That night, she left the retirement home behind her as she glided forward back to her home, worried and broken about what was to come of her mother.

Chapter 5

The forks and knives made soft clinking noises against the fine chinaware. This was more than just dinner. It was a meeting of the minds.

Agnus grabbed the serving bowl from the kitchen counter with a freshly prepared Caesar salad. The dining room chandelier shined against the parmesan flakes as she set it carefully in the middle of the table. This was the last piece of the large spread. Agnus returned to her seat on the farthest end, next to Harold, who sat at the head of the table.

Across Agnus sat her daughter, Georgianne. A beautiful young lady with a sweet spirit, she favors her mother not only in looks but also in disposition, as do her grandmother and Aunt Arlene. Just recently, she had agreed to go to church with Arlene and made a private commitment to serve the Lord. She had always known of God, but living in her home with her mother and father made the concept of God shallow. It was more of a title than a relationship. Something to talk about around holidays with her extended family. Another one of her mother's feeble attempts to stay relevant.

She loved her mother but never quite connected to her, and she could not understand why. She assumed it had something to do with her own compassion for others. Her mother cared about others, but it was typically connected to what she could get out of the relationship.

At the other end of the table, opposite Harold, was Michael, Georgianne's fiancé. He was a shrewd businessman raised among the elite of society. His father was a well-known banker who was loved by his community. His mother was a beautiful trophy wife. He attended the local private school with high tuition and even higher Romanesque buildings. Georgianne had met him during her first year in college. The two found a ton in common, given their parentage. The relationship was almost mandatory. Her mother and father swooned over Michael when they met him, and Georgianne was convinced it was meant to be. Michael was a sharp dresser who always wore long-sleeved business shirts. His hands were clean, and his nails were well-manicured. But Georgianne knew a special secret about her soon-to-be-husband. A tattoo filled the skin just above his right wrist underneath the freshly pressed cotton. It was a small fish that he had gotten after graduating high school. She had seen it first while they were swimming in the lake on a weekend. He paid close attention to keeping it hidden in daylight. Michael explained that he had gotten it when he was younger, shortly after his dad passed.

"He was a Christian," he told her. "I really missed him, so I got this in his memory. I was young and stupid."

Georgianne disagreed. She loved this story. She was not active in the church when he first told her, but now that her heart was transforming, it meant so much more. It was like she knew what he had hidden deeply. It was both sad and comforting at the same time. A small piece of humility amongst all his hubris.

After scooping a large pile of Romaine and croutons onto his plate, Michael took a swig from his wine glass and cleared his throat.

"So, when do we start?" he asked, almost too loudly. Agnus and Harold both jumped in their seats at the interruption.

"What do you mean?" Agnus responded. Her eyes were bulging in his direction. She was not a fan of the question.

"Um, when do we start?" Michael responded. He glanced at Georgianne, who looked at him puzzlingly. "Eating."

Harold cleared his throat. "Now, son. We start now."

Georgianne rolled her eyes. She loved her fiancé, but he had a knack for shoving his foot in his mouth at times. What kind of question was this? Was he looking for permission?

"So, Georgianne," Agnus started, changing the subject drastically. "How's school?"

"It's fine," Georgianne responded. "I have kept my A's this semester. All I have to do now is complete the final, and I am a senior."

Agnus smiled. Georgianne grabbed a fork full of salad and ate. She did not smile back.

"Well, that's great, honey," Agnus continued. "I'm so proud of you."

Georgianne offered her first smile of the evening. She had been wrestling for months about what she would do with her life. Since the day she sat in the church that evening with her Aunt Arlene, she had felt a transformation in her heart. Suddenly, her desire to "continue the family legacy" and join finance had been replaced with a heavy burden. Something that called her in a new direction.

But, of course, she would not tell her parents that. Instead, she would finish the education they paid for and figure it out later on her own.

Harold spoke up.

"Michael, what about you? How's work?"

"It's fine," Michael responded between bites. "Little slow in the procurement area, but I have a lead that should net enough value for a fat quarterly payout."

"Ah," Harold responded. He beamed with pride. "Good for you."

"Yeah," Michael continued. "So far, I have surpassed my onboarding partner in the firm. There is talk that I could make VP by the end of the year."

"I remember when I made salesman of the quarter," Harold reminisced. "They gave me a plaque. I looked for a pay raise, but they told me to go out and make a sale. That was my prize!"

Harold laughed at his joke, and Michael chuckled softly. Georgianne and Agnus rolled their eyes. This type of crosstalk had become common. Harold had found a kindred spirit with Michael. Georgianne was not entirely sure that was a good thing, but at least it made things less awkward.

"Georgie, do you still have that study date planned for tonight?" Agnus inquired.

"I do. Ashley from class will be here in the next few to pick me up."

"Great!"

Great? Georgianne thought. Her parents were acting strangely. How was that great?

On cue, the doorbell rang. Georgianne wiped her mouth with her napkin and stood up.

"I'll get it," she said.

Ashley, a young girl from Georgianne's class, appeared in the doorway. Georgianne welcomed her in and made her way back to the table. She reached around and hugged Michael behind.

"I'm going to go ahead and leave if that's okay," she asked at the table.

"That's fine, dear," Agnus said. "Study hard!"

"Will you be okay here without me?" she asked Michael with a small smirk.

"I'll be fine," Michael responded, returning with his own smile.

In a flash, Georgianne escaped the quiet dining room and went to her friend's car. Once the headlights disappeared from the front windows, Harold grabbed his napkin and wiped his mouth. Agnus went to the windows and pulled the blinds closed.

"Okay," she began. "Now we can talk about it."

She shot a mean glance at Michael, who slowly bent his head.

"I'm sorry," he said. "I forget we don't want Georgie to know."

"Georgianne is a sweet girl. She loves her grandmother. I doubt she would approve of what we are doing. Not that we need that," explained Agnus.

"Let's get on with it," Harold spoke up. The whole idea made him uncomfortable. "Do you have everything you need, son?"

"I do," answered Michael. "It's simple really, I'll just—"

"Stop," Agnus interjected. "We do not need to rehash this. You have what you need. Now, do it quietly. The quicker we accomplish this, the quicker we can be rid of the roadblock and acquire the wealth I deserve."

Harold looked at his wife sharply.

"*We* deserve," she corrected. "I have a birthright to my family's fortune. I deserve what my father built. I love my mother, but she insists on giving it to those who have earned less. It is not fair. When this is done, I will decide who can have what. It is the way it should be."

"I have a question," Michael asked.

"Go ahead," Harold answered.

"What if she finds out I did it? I mean, she does know who I am."

"She's only met you twice," Agnus stated. "And, thankfully, her memory is fading. If she becomes wise, we will deny it. It is our word against hers."

"And you're sure this is how you want to do this?" Harold asked, staring again at his wife. "There are laws protecting people against this sort of..."

"I'm dead sure, Harold," Agnus responded with a fiery look in her eyes. "Now stop worrying about this and get it done."

With that, she stood up and collected the men's plates. She receded to the kitchen in a flash, where she started a load of dishes.

Chapter 6

"God does not forsake us," the pastor explained. "He's our ever-present help in time of need!"

Phyllis nodded her head as she watched her pastor through the recording on her phone. Thankfully, her inability to attend church had not impeded her ability to watch. Just a couple of months ago, her church had sent a young volunteer to her home and helped her access the live-streamed services on her phone. At first, it seemed like an impossible task. But, thankfully, with help from her granddaughters, she had learned enough to watch the service after the fact.

Today was no different. Leaning in her recliner, she held the phone steady with one hand and cradled her Bible in the other.

"But how do we know it's Him?" the pastor continued. "How do we recognize the voice of God in our lives?"

Phyllis perked up. This was the same question she had asked herself just days before.

"God speaks to His children through His word. He speaks to His children through their hearts. It is not about Him speaking loud enough. It is about you choosing to listen to Him over the voices of this world."

It was clarity. Phyllis wiped a tear from the corner of her eyes. *It is about choosing Him over the world.* This was something she had done since she was a small child. God had always remained at the center of her life. Lately, though, she has been feeling as if something is wrong in her life. It was as though her heart was filled with unrest. She kept asking if it was God but was not sure. She had brought it up to her daughter multiple times.

Arlene had reassured her she was okay. Agnus had reminded her she was not.

But what was God trying to tell her? It was a question she needed to focus on. She needed to pray about it.

Phyllis placed her teacup on the small nightstand next to her chair. She felt her mind start to swim again.

Right on cue, she thought. The episodes were getting worse. It seemed with each passing day, she would find herself increasingly confused and dizzy in the evenings.

"Jesus, help me," she whispered. "Please, Lord, help me."

Turning off her phone, she adjusted the seat and pushed the reclined legrest back underneath. It was time to head to bed. The large clock on the wall in front of her showed

6:47. She remembered when she was able to stay up past nine on most days. Now, she would be lucky to make it past 7.

With a steady hand on her cane, she leaned forward and pulled herself up to her feet. The floor shifted slightly beneath her feet, and she stumbled back down to the chair once again. After a quick breath in, she tried again. This time, she was able to stand upright. Leaning heavily on her cane, she shuffled forward towards her bedroom.

Before she made it to the bedroom, a quick, dark movement caught the corner of her eye. She stopped and quickly turned to see behind her, but only her dark kitchen remained.

"Hmm," she mumbled. "These meds are driving me crazy."

As she turned slowly back, she heard a small metallic sound from behind her. Her body stiffened as her mind raced to try and guess what it could be. *Did something fall? Was it the AC?* The thoughts bounced quickly as her heart rate climbed.

As quietly as she could, she slowly turned her body around to get a glimpse.

Her heart pounded in her chest. Before her, partly shrouded in the darkness, was a tall figure dressed in black. It had a mask on that covered everything but its eyes. By the height, she quickly assumed it was a man. The body was slender, and the legs wore tightly fitted sweatpants. The man was wearing a long-sleeve, black sweatshirt, and in his right hand was a baseball bat.

Her mouth dropped. This was the same figure from her backyard.

Phyllis could not speak. All she could do was let out a cry of despair. The masked man stepped closer to her, taunting her. He lifted the metal baseball bat and firmly bounced it in quick, separated rhythms on his left palm. The noise was deafening.

Phyllis felt her eyesight narrowing. Her senses were sharpening as the adrenaline coursed through her veins. Her heart was maniacal in her chest, to the point she felt her rib cage bruising.

"Dear Jesus, dear Jesus," was all she could mutter.

The man was perfectly silent. Falling backward in fear as the man stepped closer again, her cane fell out from underneath her, and she slid down the wall next to her bedroom door.

"Please!" she shouted. "Please! Don't hurt me! I have nothing!"

The man said nothing still. Closer, he approached until he was standing nearly over her. He leaned forward and reached the bat out over Phyllis' head. She watched as his long arm extended. She scanned the black sleeve, tracing out the wrinkles in his sweater against the dark ceiling. Her eyes slowly combed down the long arm, taking in every detail.

In her panic, images flashed before her eyes. Still shots of her family and her children. Then her mind switched to images of church and Christ. She saw paintings of Jesus she had longed marveled at and symbols of her belief on bumper stickers and church windows.

"Jesus, save me!"

The man appeared startled. His arm flinched as he pulled the bat towards him while he stepped backward. Phyllis saw this as an opportunity to get back up and make a run for it. Though her body ached with age and her mind swam as usual, the adrenaline in her blood pushed her forward with a renewed vigor and sharpened her senses just enough for action.

She darted for the back door, the room still spinning. As she pushed open the glass, she peered over her shoulder again. The man had not moved from the living room. He was still standing there, watching her.

Phyllis backed out onto the slender patio until her legs met rod iron. The man tilted his head and slowly approached her, still swinging the bat. Phyllis had nowhere to go. The rod iron gate buried itself into her upper thighs as she lurched backward, trying to escape the oncoming intruder. The dark figure dropped the bat and bolted in her direction, arms outstretched. Phyllis's mind tilted to the right, causing her whole body to tilt with it. With one quick movement, her upper body leaned too far over the railing, and she fell backward, headfirst to the asphalt ground beneath her.

The final image she saw before entering Glory was the masked face of the intruder as he looked after her fall.

Chapter 7

Arlene's hands trembled more vigorously than usual as she reached for her purse on the counter. Just moments before, she received a call from Agnus. It still had not made sense.

"She killed herself, Arlene," Agnus explained.

No, that is impossible. Her mother was a born-again believer. She treasured her old age and the sanctity of life. She would have *never* committed suicide.

The Uber door shut behind her, and the driver pulled away.

What if, she thought. *What if she did?*

It was the slightest of possibilities, but it was still possible. Her mother's mental health was deteriorating rapidly. Just a few nights ago, she mentioned the intruder again to Arlene. Told her about the man who followed her from her backyard. She had said she was worried he would show up at her apartment now.

"Of course not, Mom," Arlene had reassured her. "How would he even know where you lived?"

It did not seem to console her. Phyllis was certain God was warning her about something. Something evil.

The driver pulled up to the retirement home, where police officers and ambulances dotted the grass in the front yard. This was the final straw. Like a dam bursting, Arlene broke down, still sitting in the car. The driver, a compassionate man, sat still and offered a concerned glance into the rearview mirror.

"Ma'am," he offered. "Can I help you? Do you need anything?"

"No, thank you," Arlene responded between broken sighs. "I'm fine."

With a heavier struggle than usual, she managed to escape the backseat and hobbled up the stone steps toward the first officer. After a quick explanation and verification that she was a daughter to the deceased, the officers escorted her through the front door and up to the apartment. The room was cluttered with forensic bags and caution tape. Nearly a dozen officers and investigators traced different rooms of the apartment. In the kitchen stood Agnus, Harold, and Georgianne.

Allison has not made it, thought Arlene. Her daughter must be rushing from school to get here. *Jesus, protect my baby.*

Arlene watched as Agnus studied the kitchen counter with her back turned. Her shoulders were shaking slightly. Was her sister crying?

That would be a first in a while, thought Arlene.

"Ma'am!" a voice shouted from behind Arlene, startling her.

From around her shoulder, an investigator in a blue jacket made his way to the kitchen, heading towards Agnus. It was then that Arlene recognized the sound of water at the kitchen sink.

Of course, she thought. *Agnus is always cleaning.*

Agnus turned abruptly and faced the investigator. In her right hand was a coffee cup.

"Ma'am," said the investigator again. "Please do not clean anything. We have not swept that area yet."

"There was a dirty cup in the sink. I can't stand dirty dishes," explained Agnus.

Arlene could tell that her sister was slightly manic by the pain of it all. If not, irrational. It was an unfamiliar trait for Agnus, but mourning has a funny way of breaking down walls in people.

The investigator softly reached out and grabbed the cup with a gloved hand. As he placed it gingerly into an evidence bag, he nodded his head.

"I'm sure, ma'am," he softly answered. "I know this is tough. I am sorry for your loss."

The investigator retreated quickly from the kitchen with the bagged cup and left the family alone again.

"Hey, Aggie," Arlene whispered. Her sister turned to face her. Her face hardened once again.

"Hey, Arlene," Agnus spoke up.

Her voice carried a more compassionate tone than normal. It was slightly jarring. Arlene couldn't remember the last time she heard her sister break her tough façade. But there's nothing quite like losing a parent that will soften even the hardest of hearts.

Arlene's eyes were filled to the brim with tears. She could see that Agnus had smeared makeup streaks on each cheek. Another anomaly. *God bless her.*

"Hey, Aggie," Arlene whispered as she embraced her sister. "Hey, Harold."

Georgianne stepped forward and grabbed hold of her aunt. She hugged her deeply. There had always been a softness between the two. Arlene saw a lot of her daughter in her niece.

"Hey, baby girl," she whispered in Georgianne's ear. "I'm so sorry."

"*I'm* sorry," Georgianne responded. "I can't imagine."

"She loved us all. We are all hurting. But she's in Glory now."

Agnus turned abruptly and hid her face. Thoughts of heaven and Jesus often made her uncomfortable. Arlene was thankful that she kept her opinions quiet during this moment.

"Have we heard anything from the investigators?" Arlene asked as Georgianne stepped away and held her arms tightly around her chest.

"We just spoke with Detective Thomas right before you showed up. He's out back right now," Harold explained.

"What did he say?"

"They are calling it a suicide," Agnus answered from the kitchen. "She had another episode while we were away and jumped from the balcony. It is the only thing that makes sense."

"I just can't believe that mom would do this," Arlene whispered. "This isn't her."

Agnus became frustrated. "I have told you a million times, Arlene. These mental episodes have gotten worse over the past few weeks. It felt like we were constantly calming her down every time we came by. She was paranoid about everything, thinking people were after her. I feel like this was the ultimate step."

The words stung like razor blades. Arlene tamped down the urge to correct her sister. She knew she was hurting like herself. Everyone manages pain differently. Her sister just does it with more hurt.

"She was a Christian, Aggie. She loved her life. I cannot imagine she would—"

"Arlene, I know you are upset," Agnus interrupted. "I am, too. But you need to come back down to reality right now. Our mother was sick. She was dying. She was not in her right mind. This is why I *insisted* on the Power of Attorney a while back. I saw the writing on the wall."

Harold stepped forward and put his hands on his wife's shoulders. Agnus bit her lip and tucked the final words in her sentence back into her holster. Enough was said.

"I'd like to talk with the investigator," Arlene answered softly.

A few minutes later, a man dressed in oversized slacks, a white shirt, and a black tie approached the group. He sported a thick 5 o'clock shadow, and his hair was combed haphazardly. He was all business, with little to no time for personal appearances.

"Detective Thomas?" Arlene asked.

"Yes," he replied, turning to find Arlene sitting on a stool near the kitchen bar.

"I'm Arlene, Phyllis' daughter."

"Ah, yes, your sister mentioned you would be here. I am sorry for your loss."

"Thank you," Arlene answered politely. "My sister and brother-in-law mentioned that your team is calling this a suicide?"

"At this time, that's correct," he replied quickly. Then, as if he remembered who he was talking to, he tried his best to soften. "All signs point to that conclusion, unfortunately. So far, we have not seen any signs of forced entry or a struggle. The only thing we saw was an empty pill bottle on the kitchen counter and smears on the back sliding glass. We, of course, need to run prints, but it seems as if the smears belonged to your mother. Our guess is she took too many pills and...," he paused. "...carried out the rest of what happened."

"What pills were in the bottle?" Arlene asked.

"We are running tests to confirm, but…"

"It's the medication her doctor prescribed," Agnus interjected. "I saw the bottle. It's what she takes normally. *Levodopa.* Her doctor had mentioned she showed signs of onset Parkinson's, and she started taking it a few months back. I have been the one to give it to her."

"Are you aware of any side effects?"

"The doctor said too much could lead to bits of psychosis and discomfort," Agnus explained. "But I manage her meds, so we've avoided that. She's not supposed to take it without me here. She must've gotten into them when I wasn't here."

"I'm no doctor, but my guess is if she took too much of that, she could have had a psychotic break. That would explain what we are seeing here," the detective opined.

"Parkinson's?" Arlene asked, trying to catch up. "I never knew…"

"I told you," Agnus interrupted. "You probably forgot. You have got enough to worry about."

Another stinger. It was no secret that Arlene's ALS symptoms had increased. But she was still her mother's daughter. She wished she had paid more attention.

Detective Thomas grabbed a white card with his name and badge number from his shirt pocket and handed it to Arlene. He grabbed two more and handed them each to Agnus and Harold.

"We are working this case hard to get answers," he reassured. "If you think of anything that may help us, please reach out. We want to rule out everything before we make a final decision. Call me night or day."

"Thank you, detective," Agnus responded. She smiled and shoved the card into her purse on the counter.

Detective Thomas nodded his head and retreated back to the patio where he continued his investigation. Arlene wiped more tears from her eyes.

"Arlene, you need to go back home. This is too much for you," Agnus explained.

"No, Allison is on her way. I'll wait for her to get here."

"Fine," Agnus responded. "Harold, take Georgianne back home. I'm going to stay here until the investigators leave. Georgianne, have you called Michael?"

"I left him a voicemail, but he hasn't answered. I have no clue where he is right now."

Agnus shot a glance at Harold before turning back to her daughter.

"I'm sure he'll get here as soon as he can, dear. He's probably busy at work."

Georgianne did not respond. In her mind, there was nothing more important than being here, right now, at this moment. It made no sense why her future husband did not share the same.

Harold and Georgianne left a few moments later, and Arlene sat quietly on the stool, sniffling and wiping her leaking emotion from her cheeks. Soon, her daughter would arrive. Arlene was certain she would be devastated. Allison had always loved her grandmother. When she was younger, Phyllis would insist on taking her to Sunday School in the mornings. Of course, Arlene happily obliged. This started a longstanding closeness between them both. At the center was Jesus. It was a beautiful thing to witness.

"How far is Allison?" Agnus asked, still standing in the kitchen near the sink.

"I'm not sure," Arlene responded. "I'm so worried about her."

Across town, a young woman gripped her steering wheel in anguish as she focused on the road before her. Her swollen eyes made it a challenge to see, but her heart was leading the way. Somewhere across town, the body of her hero lay cold and dead.

Allison struggled not to question God.

"Lord, why? Why would you take her like this?"

Her car rounded the corner of her grandmother's retirement home. The red and blue lights stood as warning signs of what was to come.

Part 2: The Truth Shall Set You Free

"... Behold, you have sinned against the Lord, and be sure your sin will find you out."

Numbers 32:23

Chapter 8

The first thing Phyllis felt was warmth. An inviting, glorious warmth that felt like soft light wrapped around her body. She was comfortable, relaxed, and serene.

She was not entirely certain of what had happened. Only that she had fallen from her balcony and awoken in this...*place?* No, it was more than a place. It was a feeling. An experience.

A physical happiness.

Her words escaped her. She had nothing to say. As she scanned her surroundings, she could not make out any figures or landmarks. It was just wisps of cool currents and a soft buzz of melody. One that had no origin. Only infinite joy.

Heaven? she thought to herself quietly. Something inside her beckoned her to remain still. Silent. Reserved.

"Yes," a voice answered.

It was just louder than a whisper. It felt as if whoever was talking was right beside her and far away—all at the same time.

"Welcome home, child," the voice continued. "I've been waiting for you, Phyllis."

Who-? Her thoughts began.

"I am."

It was an ambiguous answer, yet it made perfect sense. Phyllis recognized the voice. This was—*I am.*

"Child, you have fought the good fight. You have kept your faith. You have remained a servant of the Most High."

The 'Most High,' Phyllis repeated without speaking. She stood to her feet amidst the clouds and light. Immediately, she realized the pain she had grown accustomed to was gone. She scanned her body. The wrinkles had disappeared. Her skin was clear, fresh, and new. Her pores seemed to exude light, giving a soft, golden glow about her body. She was illuminated, elevated, and restored all at once.

Finally, her voice was available. In a soft tone, she spoke.

"Father?"

"Yes child," he responded. His voice is even closer now. The words held their own individual echoes. Each syllable sounded like the rushing of a babbling brook. Not loud, but calm, and powerful. Phyllis could tell that that voice held the highest of powers but possessed the deepest of mercy.

"Am I dead?"

"What was once dead and gone is now alive forevermore."

"Am I in Heaven?"

"You are with your Heavenly Father, Phyllis."

"How did I die?"

Silence. Phyllis waited patiently. Though the response hadn't come, she knew the speaker remained. It was a tangible presence, unlike anything she had ever experienced. He was both beside her and within her, all at the same time.

"Your life was taken from you, Phyllis. The schemes of the wicked prevailed on Earth, but your soul rests with me, child."

"Why?" Phyllis answered. She didn't cry. She wasn't sad. But her curiosity remained.

"The root of so many evils, Phyllis. The most wicked of man's creation."

It was clear. Phyllis needed no further explanation. Her life ended on Earth because of money. Her story was snuffed out early because of greed.

Pity, she thought.

"For them, child," the Father answered. "But for you, glory awaits."

Chapter 9

Allison's toes felt scrunched in her new heels. She only had flats when her grandmother passed and felt it wasn't enough to be underdressed for such a wonderful woman's memorial. She purchased the heels from a nearby store not hours before she arrived at the church. They weren't worn in, and she was certain the right heel still had a tag in the inserts.

But she kept it to herself. After all, this wasn't about her. And the last thing her mother needed to hear was her daughter complaining about her shoes.

"Hey, mama," she whispered into Arlene's ear as she bent behind the pew.

Her mother turned towards her, dried tear stains underlining her eyes and a crumpled-up napkin in the palm of her left hand.

"Hey there, love," Arlene whispered back as she pressed her cheek against her daughter.

Their embrace lingered for a few moments. Out of the corner of her eye stood her Aunt Agnus. She was dressed in a black power skirt suit. White pearl buttons traced her diaphragm and settled on a thin white belt that outlined her waist. On her feet were two black flats.

Of course, Allison muttered to herself. Her aunt was not much for respect, especially when it came to her mother. No, the only person that Aunt Aggie ever fully respected was herself. And she demanded others to do the same through intimidation and even threats.

Stop it, Allison, she whispered under her breath. *She is mourning like everyone else.*

It had only been a year since Allison had made her decision to follow Christ. Old habits of negativity and disdain for others were hard to break.

"Hey, Aunt Aggie."

"Hey, Allison," Agnus answered. She leaned in and side-hugged her niece.

That was enough. Agnus returned to standing watch over her mother's casket, and Allison found her seat next to Arlene. The service was to start in just a few.

People continued to file in sporadically over the next half hour. Friends and relatives, previous coworkers and neighbors. Allison only recognized a handful, but her mother seemed to know everybody.

Behind her mother and next to her aunt were her two uncles. Phyllis' sons were tall men with weathered faces and tightly pressed suits. Allison had never really gotten close to them. They left for out of state not long after she was born. Occasionally, she'd see them around holidays and for special occasions, but as quickly as they arrived, they left. And with them, Allison's cousins. This made her sad for a moment. But of course, everything was sad in this place.

Finally, a shorter man with dark, black hair approached Agnus and shook her hand. He spoke a few kind words to her and then searched the front pews for a familiar face. When she found Arlene, he smiled warmly and approached. Arlene smiled back and extended her hand.

"Hey there, Mr. Taylor," she offered.

"Please, Arlene. Call me Douglas," he responded kindly. "I knew Mrs. Phyllis for decades. She was a close friend of mine. So was your father."

"She spoke very kindly of you," Arlene responded. "She always said you were one of the smartest attorneys in the city."

Douglas smiled. "Well, I don't know about that. But I sure appreciate it."

He paused for a second. It looked like he was deciding whether to say the next sentence.

"Arlene," he started. After a quick look around, he sat gingerly beside her and leaned in. "I know now is not the right time, but I'm not sure when I will see you again after the funeral. I need to discuss something with you at your earliest convenience. Something regarding your mother's affairs."

"Of course," Arlene responded. "Anything for family."

The two shared a knowing smile. Douglas nodded his head slightly and returned to his seat towards the back of the auditorium. Allison was puzzled by the interaction.

"Who was that, mom?" she asked.

"Douglas Taylor," Arlene answered. "Mom and Dad's lifelong friend. Your grandfather did some work with him a while back when he owned his construction company. Ever since then, they would always use him for advice."

"I thought Aunt Aggie mentioned Mr. Goldstein was the family lawyer."

"He is. Douglas was just a friend with good advice."

"Then why would he need to talk to you about Grandmother's affairs?"

Silence. Arlene hadn't thought that deeply into it. She figured it was just a friendly chat about what the family should and shouldn't do. But now that Allison brought it up, it did seem strange. What would Douglas Taylor have to do with anything regarding the family estate? And if he did, wouldn't that go through Aggie? She had taken over her mother's interests a few months back. *Everything* went through her. The sale of the home, her mother's new apartment in the retirement community. Even her mother's medical care. *All of it.*

The music began as a slideshow, sharing pictures of Phyllis' life. Tears flowed and the sanctuary filled with sniffles and muffled cries. The story of a wonderful woman bought and saved by grace, took up the next hour and a half as the pastor shared a heartfelt eulogy about his longstanding member.

Arlene patted her eyes to avoid further smearing her mascara as her daughter gripped her hands tightly. From somewhere deep down inside her, she thought she could hear a whisper.

"Welcome home, my child."

Chapter 10

Douglas Taylor's office was small and quaint. The furniture was neat and clean, but it was obvious that they had filled this office space for decades. The walls were adorned with pictures of farms and woodlands. Above Arlene's head was a portrait of a smiling family made up of two adult daughters, their children, and an elderly woman's center frame. Everyone was happy. It was as if everything was under control. Decisions were clear, and all they had to do was focus on living their life to the fullest.

I miss you, Mom, thought Arlene. *I wish you were here.*

"Arlene?" a woman at the receptionist's desk asked.

"That's me."

"Mr. Taylor, will you see you now," she added with a smile.

Arlene gripped the chair armrests firmly with her right hand and leaned on her cane with her left. Slowly, she stood up and made her way into the office adjacent to the waiting room. Directly across from her stood Douglas, dressed in the same suit he wore to her mother's funeral. He immediately walked towards the door and offered Arlene a chair.

"Hey, Arlene," he began. "How are you holding up?"

"I'm okay," Arlene replied. "Still sad, of course, but I know she's in a better place."

"Absolutely," Douglas responded. "I can only imagine the meeting in heaven when Phyllis opened her eyes that day. What a thought."

Douglas lifted his eyes slightly as if he were trying to picture Glory. He smiled and returned his gaze to Arlene as he sat down. The smile quickly faded.

"Arlene, thank you so much for swinging by today. I would not normally have you come here so soon as after your mother passing if it wasn't urgent."

"It's no problem."

"Arlene, are you aware of your mother's—" he paused. "Are you aware of your mother's financial affairs?"

"I know that she had quite a bit left over from Dad's business. And assuming the sale of the home was as big as Agnus described, I would guess there was more there as well."

Douglas' eyes widened. "She sold her home?"

"Well, Agnus sold it," Arlene explained. "She took over as mom's power of attorney a few months ago when her episodes started.

This concerned Douglas; Arlene could tell. He leaned back into his chair and sighed softly.

"This is why I wanted you to come in," he said. "Instead of Agnus."

"What is this about?"

"Arlene, your mother called me about a week before her death. She told me she had given you something to hold on to. A letter?"

Arlene suddenly remembered the letter. With everything that had happened in the past couple weeks, she had forgotten she had it. To this day, she hasn't opened it.

"She did, but I haven't read it yet."

Douglas was shocked. "Do you still have it?"

"I do. It's back at my house."

"Good," Douglas explained. "When you go home, I want you to make sure it's put somewhere safe. Somewhere, no one can ever find it without your permission."

"What is it?"

"It's a copy of your mother's will."

"Why would I need that?" asked Arlene. "Wouldn't that need to go to Aggie? She is the executor."

Silence. Douglas pushed back his chair and stood up with his hands firmly folded behind his back. He was watching his words carefully now.

"Arlene, were you there when Agnus took over POA for your mother?"

"No. I found out about it after the fact."

Douglas stopped and turned towards Arlene. He then shifted to the front of his desk and took the seat closest to her. With a look of worry on his face, he stared deeply into Arlene's eyes.

"Arlene, I do not believe your mother was paranoid. And I do not believe your mother committed suicide."

"I'm sorry?" Arlene's mouth was agape. What on Earth was Douglas talking about?

"Four months ago, your mother approached me in secret to adjust her last will and testament. She said she wanted to keep it under the radar and away from your family's lawyer. I didn't question it too much as I've always held such great respect for your parents. But—"

He stopped again. Arlene leaned forward and nodded as if to silently permit for him to continue.

"Arlene, your mother informed me of a separate account that your father had left her when he passed. A trust account under the name of his business. It was a high-yield investment account worth more than 15 million dollars. It had been a secret retirement plan that he and your mother held. Because the tax ID for the trust was different from your family's, it flew under your sister's radar when she took over as POA."

"15 million dollars?" Arlene was stunned.

"And counting," Douglas added. "But that's not all."

What on Earth else could there be? Thought Arlene. Her mind was swimming.

"There is only one trustee listed," Douglas said as he leaned in. "You."

The room tilted quickly and then corrected itself before Arlene could pass out. *15 million dollars?* She couldn't understand it. Why would she be the only child of her family of six to have access to this money? What was her mother trying to tell her?

"What does that mean?" Arlene asked.

"It means that in the eyes of the court, only you have a rightful claim to the money now that your mother has passed. And the way it was written, this was always the case."

Arlene left the office and made her way home via the bus. The whole time she played the conversation over in her head.

Secret account.

15 million dollars.

Only you.

"God," she whispered. "What are You trying to tell me here?"

Nothing. She knew He heard her. It was something she had known her whole life. And she also knew that sometimes, no answer at all was the answer she needed.

"Sometimes, God rests in the silence, Arlene," her mother had told her once. "He always speaks. We just have to listen."

"I'm listening, mama," Arlene whispered out loud. "God, speak to me."

The bus turned sharply to the left, causing Arlene's cane to shift in the seat next to her. Instinctively, she reached out and grabbed it before it fell to the floor beneath her. As the bus straightened up again, she pulled the cane close to her. The wooden handle jammed between the two seats and her purse. With a tug, she pulled the cane free, and the purse pushed forward, laying on the seat. Arlene noticed a white envelope peeking out from atop her purse.

My mother's letter.

It couldn't be. She was certain she had placed that in her mail basket at home next to her front door. She reached and grabbed it. Sure enough, the letter was addressed to her in her mother's handwriting. She realized she had carried it the whole time, since that night at her mother's new apartment.

She opened it and pulled out a stack of papers. Stapled together was a packet of continued legal jargon with a bold title that read:

Rock Construction Company Trust

It was named after her father's construction company. Beneath the packet was a loose sheet of paper. A letter written in her mother's hand. She pulled it to the top and read it to herself.

My sweet Arlene,

Enclosed is a copy of your father and my trust. This has been ratified, created, and confirmed. The value is great, and every bit of it is yours. I know this will be a shock for you to realize, but with this money, you and Allison will never have to worry again. It was what your father wanted, and it's what I want for you.

I understand that after I die, this may cause friction between you and Agnus and your brothers. But these are my wishes. Take this money and do whatever you can to live comfortably. Pay your medical bills, receive the best treatment, and cancel your debt. And provide for Allison. She has a heart for ministry. She has told me so. Give her every opportunity to pursue what she is called to pursue.

Never forget, my love. God speaks in various ways. Just listen.

Mom

Tears fell on the page in her lap. Her life was changed forever. With this money, she had access to the medical help she needed to push back the effects of her disease. Her daughter had the money she needed to pursue ministry. She smiled and sighed.

Then, as quickly as she relaxed, she felt the hair stick up on her arms. Suddenly, she remembered what else Douglas said.

I don't believe your mother was paranoid. And I don't believe she committed suicide.

Why? Why didn't he believe it? The truth is, she didn't either. Something didn't add up. Her mother was a firm believer in the sanctity of life. She treasured her time on this Earth. Sure, she longed for heaven—to see her father again—but she knew the pain it would cause to leave in such a way. *Suicide?* No, that wasn't Phyllis.

So, then, why did Douglas—and Arlene—sense something else happened? Why was this money handled in secrecy? Why not share it with her brothers and sister? There was plenty of it. What was the point of hiding it?

And why was her mother worried about her safety? Was she being followed? Was there something more sinister happening?

The bus came to a stop at the bus stop near her home. She tucked the packet of paper and letter back into the envelope and shoved it back into her purse. Her fear gave way to emboldened anger. Someone hurt her mother. She was certain of it.

I'm listening, God, she thought. *Keep talking.*

Chapter 11

Agnus rubbed the check between her fingers. Her blood pressure was pumped at an elevated rate. She was excited.

The bank doors closed behind her as she waltzed straight to the teller line. Her demeanor screamed that of a woman in charge.

"I need to see a banker," she chirped. "Now."

She raised her hand to show the check to the teller. From a distance, the teller could make out more zeros than typical.

"Of course," she answered. "Right away."

From behind Agnus, Michael appeared. He was dressed in his suit, and the badge on his chest told the world he was a premier investment broker with a fancy office at the corner of the bank.

"Agnus, we need to talk," he whispered.

"Not now, Michael. I'm busy."

She kept facing forward. What she had to deposit was more than what Michael handled. He was a small-time investment banker. This money was made for bank managers.

"Agnus, I can't sleep. This is eating me---,"

Agnus turned sharply and leaned into Michael.

"I don't care," she retorted. "You agreed to help us. Now we are here. What is done is done. Grow up, move on, and take your share."

Michael's face was pale white. The secret he carried was draining all the color from his skin. Agnus took in his expression and rolled her eyes.

"Pull yourself together," she jabbed and then turned to face the bank manager who approached them both.

Agnus disappeared into the banker's office, and Michael was left staring into the bank lobby. After a few minutes, he went back to his office and closed the door.

The bank manager was a tall man whose impression screamed high class. He pulled out a desk chair and offered it to Agnus.

"Give me a moment, please," Agnus asked. She pulled out her cell phone. "I'm going to call my lawyer."

With Goldstein on the phone, the three of them conducted a full transfer of Phyllis' affairs into a joint account for Agnus and Harold. The total sum provided was $1.5 million. This included a million in total assets from the family estate and another $500,000 from the sale of Phyllis' home. Agnus, as the acting executor of the estate, was given the will by

Goldstein left behind, which dictated an equal share to the remaining children. Broken down, the estate was divided into four sets of $375,000.

On speaker, Goldstein piped up, "The sale of the house was not included in the will. This means that whoever possessed control of its sale would own the amount. That means the full value sold will remain with Agnus."

The banker's eyebrows twitched. This didn't make sense. *Surely, the house was divided between the children.*

Agnus lifted her chin and smiled. Reluctantly, the full $875,000 was transferred over into Agnus' account. The remaining $1.1 million was left in the estate, ready to be written in checks for Phyllis' children.

Agnus shook the banker's hand and stood up abruptly. Without a word, she turned and left. Her account was filled to the brim, and all the proceeds from the home were hers. The plan had worked. She took the lion's share of her family's estate and, with the help of her lawyer, had an airtight plan.

No one could stop her.

At his desk, Michael rolled up his cotton sleeves and dragged his well-manicured fingers through his now-disheveled hair. He locked the office door and waited in silence for some kind of answer. Instinctively, he rubbed the fish tattoo on his wrist with his thumb. His heart bounced against his chest.

In front of him was an open page on his computer. The blinking cursor beckoned him to write out his thoughts. Above the cursor were the words,

Dear Georgianne...

What am I doing? He thought. *I can't tell her what I did. It would devastate her.*

What's worse, it would *destroy* him. He was sure Georgianne loved her, but ever since she found Christ, her appetite for wrongdoing had greatly diminished. Michael had no world where she found out what he did and still chose to stay with him.

He shook his head. How could he be so stupid? Is he really more concerned with his fiancé's opinion of him than his own future? There was no turning back from this. Sooner or later, he would be found out. *Why not now?*

He rested his fingers on the keys. Slowly, deliberately, he added more words to his confession.

I don't know how to begin this. Other than that, I'm so sorry.
I'm so...

A knock on the door startled him. He quickly minimized the screen and stood to answer the door. With a hand on the handle, he sighed deeply and attempted to shake off the panic that played with his emotions.

In due time, he thought.

Clearing his throat, he unlocked the door and opened it, welcoming in his next customer.

Chapter 12

Edgar Thomas had a strict routine every morning he entered the station. First, he followed a straight line to his office midway down the long hall behind the intake desk. His door was the brown one with a worn-out kickplate at the bottom. From what he understood, the detective who held it before him made quite a few enemies in the force with his "no-nonsense" mentality. This meant many angry visits with closed fists and patent-leather shoes leaving their impression on the brass plate.

Edgar made it a point to be *less* difficult. Though he was firm in his convictions and painstakingly thorough with his cases, he tried his best to build strong relationships with the deputies at the station and the boys downtown at the courthouse. After all, his job meant calling on them all for support occasionally.

Catch more flies with honey, he reminded himself. An old adage his father taught him as a boy.

After setting his briefcase down on his desk, he walked a narrow line straight to the breakroom.

Coffee. The only thing that mattered at a time like this. He liked his black with just a sprinkle of raw sugar. It was a trick he had picked up from his years aboard the ship in the Navy. Things like creamer were in short supply, so he had conditioned himself to enjoy the bitterness of dark roast with no *fluff*. But, of course, now that he was in the labor force, he allowed himself a hint of the sweeter things in life. Not too much, though. No need to get soft.

Once his coffee was in hand, he walked back slowly toward his office, entertaining any random conversations that popped up along the way. It was his way of "staying in touch with the beat," as he put it. Many of the officers who traced this hallway came from narcotics, his old stomping grounds. Now that he was in homicide, he missed the fast pace of drug busts and shakedowns. These days, he was responding to sad scenes after the fact. Dead bodies and crimes of passion. Gang-turf wars and bloody domestic disputes. It was a different pace altogether, but he didn't mind it. His goal was simple: put in two more years and retire. After that, he would put all the creamer he wanted into his coffee and do it in silence.

His backside barely settled into the worn leather desk chair when his phone rang. He took a long swig of his coffee and set the cup on the desk. With a smooth motion, he picked up the phone and spoke clearly into the receiver.

"Taylor."

"I have an Arlene Sky here to see you."

His mind raced. The name sounded familiar, but he could not put it together. He pulled out his calendar.

"Do I have an appointment?"

"I don't see one," the receptionist responded. "She said it is regarding a Phyllis Moore?"

The suicide at the retirement home. The name stuck out. He had just buttoned up his paperwork on that case a couple of days ago. The details were still fresh in his mind. The elderly victim, roughly 85, had fallen from a third-story balcony. The coroner said she was dead on impact. Oddly enough, her tox screening showed that she had an elevated level of Levodopa in her bloodstream. A pill bottle prescribed by her physician was empty upon investigation. It was assumed she had overdosed, causing hallucinations and resulting in her taking her own life.

"Send her in."

The phone clicked on the other end. Edgar's mind raced. *Why would the daughter come to the station?* He wondered if he had missed something. Did he say something?

There was a soft knock at the door.

"Come in."

A middle-aged woman with a cane emerged, struggling to push open the door. Quickly, Edgar jumped to his feet and assisted. The cane triggered his memory. This was the daughter from the crime scene with all the questions.

"Hello, Detective Thomas," she began. "Do you remember me?"

"Yes, I do," Edgar responded. "You are the daughter from the retirement home a couple of weeks back. Moore?"

"I'm Arlene Sky, Phyllis' daughter. I was married before and had a name change."

"Ah, I see. What can I do for you, Ms. Sky?"

Arlene paused. For a moment, she used her need to get comfortable on the couch as an excuse to collect her thoughts. The whole bus ride to the station was spent rehearsing what she would say and which questions she would ask. But now that she was here, her nerves got the best of her, and everything flew out the window.

"Well, Detective," she began finally. "You had asked me to contact you if I had any more information about my mother's case."

"That's correct," Edgar confirmed. He reached into his desk and retrieved a manila folder. The tab read *P. Moore.*

"I noted down the following: "It was determined to be a suicide.". No forced entry into the apartment and no signs of a struggle minus smears on the door."

"Right," was all Arlene could say. Once again, silence.

Edgar's eyebrows furrowed. "I'm sorry, Ms. Sky, you were saying?"

"I apologize, Detective," Arlene said. "I'm just struggling to get this out."

"Take your time."

"Detective...I believe...my mother was murdered."

Edgar's eyes widened. "Why do you believe that?"

"A couple of months before my mother died, she had told me and my sister that she felt she was being followed. On a few occasions, she even talked about seeing a man dressed in black stalking her at her house. When she moved to the apartment, she even told my sister and me that she worried the man had followed her."

"What did this man look like?" asked Edgar. By now, he was writing on a notepad furiously.

"Well, that's just it," explained Arlene. "She couldn't describe him. All she said is it was a tall, slender-like figure dressed in black."

"No descriptions of his face or anything?" His writing slowed.

"Honestly, Detective. We aren't even sure if it was a man…"

Edgar stopped writing. "So…do we know if this 'stalker' was real? Or was this a hallucination?"

Arlene could see that she was losing the detective. He was nice enough to keep his true feelings hidden, but the more she talked, the less he believed her. She supposed it made sense. Even now, she was struggling to believe herself. But, when Douglas told her he felt she was murdered, the sneaking suspicion she was worried about was confirmed. Something was up, and she had to get to the bottom of it.

"I knew my mother," she began. "I knew her very well. She was old, and she was dramatic at times…but she was never crazy. I know this sounds unbelievable, but I can't help but believe her. She told me she was being followed, and she feared for her life."

The detective leaned back in his chair and stared at Arlene. She couldn't confirm it, but she felt as if he was studying her face. Checking for a lie.

"Ms. Sky," he began.

"Please, call me Arlene."

He smiled. "Okay, Arlene. Would you like a cup of coffee?"

"No, thank you."

Another sigh. Finally, the detective leaned forward and dropped his shoulders slightly.

"I've seen a lot of cases like this in my time." He pointed to her mother's file. "They never get easier. It's really sad to see life taken so abruptly. My condolences to you and your family."

Arlene gritted her teeth. Normally, she would have accepted the condolences. It was her nature. She was the timid one. The kind one. But ever since she opened that letter on the bus, she felt something shift within her. Now, instead of listening, she waited for her turn to speak.

The detective continued. "Your mother's toxicology report showed a high dose of the drug Levodopa in her bloodstream. It is consistent with the empty pill bottle your sister pointed out on the kitchen counter. As you know, the drug is a highly powerful treatment for Parkinson's disease. In overdose quantities, it is known to cause severe cases of paranoia and psychosis. We believe it was because of this overdose that your mother took her own life."

Arlene physically winced. The detective saw it and softened his approach.

"I know that is difficult to hear, Ms. Ss—Arlene. But please know that no one in this station believes your mother intentionally committed suicide. We believe, due to her age, and...," he checked his notes again. "...and due to what your sister described to us as her frequent bouts of forgetfulness and difficulties, she accidentally overdosed. And the drug did the rest of the damage."

Still nothing from Arlene.

He continued. "This would also explain her possible hallucinations with the dark figure she had been seeing."

Arlene's eyes narrowed. The words that the detective said bounced around in her head like little toy balls with nowhere to settle. *Psychosis. Hallucinations. Episodes.*

Agnus. What was she up to? Arlene whispered under her breath.

Finally, a ball of courage rose past her chest and got lodged in her throat. Before she could stop it, her mouth started speaking. Loudly.

"Detective," she announced. "Listen to me very carefully. I believe my mother's death was no accident but a well-planned murder. Someone—I am not sure who—knew where my mother lived and found out where she had moved to. They followed her there and murdered her by throwing her from her balcony. Then they made it look like suicide. I do not know how to prove it, but the Lord is my witness. I will prove it. And I am asking you to reopen this case and help me."

Edgar was astonished. This was nothing like the woman who had just hobbled into his office on her cane. The strength in her voice no longer matched the weakness she had in her body. Though he could not put his finger on it per se, the courage she had in what she just told him stoked what little reservation he may have hidden regarding the case. Though it was small, he remembered not fully understanding how a seemingly happy, intelligent woman with two doting daughters and gorgeous grandchildren suddenly threw herself to her death from her balcony. He also could not understand why a woman with no clear medical history of Parkinson's was suddenly placed on a very powerful drug whose sole purpose was to keep the symptoms of Parkinson's at bay. It did not make sense then, and now that her daughter has called him out on it, it still didn't make sense. She was on to something. Perhaps there was something far more sinister to this open-shut suicide case.

"Arlene, listen," he started. Carefully, he constructed his response in his head before he spoke. "I know you are upset, and I apologize for anything I may have said that made you feel even more hurt by what has happened. I'll admit that some details of this case don't seem to go well together. I am willing to look further at the details and see what else I can confirm for you."

A tear fell from Arlene's eye as she shifted her cane from one hand to the other. She nodded her head.

"But," he continued. "I need to warn you. We can re-look at the details of this case, but I fear that even after further investigation, we may come up short with any proof of foul play. From what I can see, even if some of the details don't make sense, it's not enough to point us towards a murderer. Your mother didn't have any cameras in her apartment, and the hallway camera down from her door was turned off just the day before her accident. I've already checked with the manager. I just want to level with you. Even after more searching, we still may be left with the same results."

Arlene nodded her head slowly. "Detective, I have lived the past few years with disappointment ever since I received my ALS diagnosis. I am a big girl. I just want to know every stone is turned over before we let this case go, and I convince myself that my godly mother who loved life was willing to kill herself."

It was enough for Edgar to go with. The request was harmless and thoughtful. Before him was a daughter who loved her mother and wanted to know the truth. And Detective Edgar Thomas was a man who staked his entire reputation on finding the truth.

Arlene shook his hand before leaving his office and closing the door behind her. For a quick moment, Edgar stared thoughtfully at the door. He walked back through the case from top to bottom. Slowly, he poured over the pictures and notes in the file. He saw the empty living room, unpacked boxes, and the smudge on the window. He pulled the picture closer to his face. There is nothing to see but hands wrestling to push the sliding glass door to the side. It had struck him odd that though the woman had just moved in, she had already chosen not to use the handle to open the door. Instead, she used her palms to push the glass sideways.

He flipped the picture over and stared at the next. It was the pill bottle. He leaned in and read the inscription carefully:

Levodopa

1200 mg dose – once daily

90 Day Supply

Edgar's eye twitched. *90-day supply? Why?* He was not a doctor, but this didn't make sense.

Quickly, he turned to his computer and typed into the internet browser. It was a simple search.

How long do you take Levodopa?

The results were endless. Various doctor entries, journals, articles, and get-well websites. They all said in different ways the same message: *You never stop taking it.* Of course not. Parkinson's is a terminal disease. Once you get it, there's typically no getting rid of it.

So, then, why would Phyllis be prescribed such a powerful drug for only a handful of months? His mind buzzed, and his heart quickened. The same old feeling he felt when he was about to break down the door of a drug dealer began to well up inside him. It was like a long-lost friend paying a visit.

He grabbed his final gulp of coffee and downed it quickly. With a flick of his wrist, he dialed the receptionist.

"Cancel all my afternoon meetings and call Agnus Palmitieri. Tell her to come down to the station. I have a few more questions regarding the P. Moore case."

He dropped the phone onto the desk and pushed back his chair. Grabbing his briefcase, he went out the door and to his car. The worn kickplate at the base of his office door caught the heel of his shoe as he turned back down the hallway and headed toward the exit. He was returning to the retirement home. It was time to determine, for the last time, if Phyllis Moore really killed herself. And his first step was to see what that hall camera was hiding the day before.

Chapter 13

Agnus furiously washed the cup and saucer from that evening's tea. Her mind was typically highly organized. All information that she processed at once was filed in separate corners. When she was ready, she would "file away" one thought, making room for another. It was precise and forward-thinking.

This night was different. The past few weeks had been different. Ever since Phyllis was found, Agnus felt her thoughts race quicker than normal. It was like everything had been pushed into overdrive. The files were scattered. And her system had been breached.

"Where do I put these?" asked Georgianne.

Agnus had to bite her lip. Her daughter had spent her whole life under Agnus' strict habits regarding the kitchen. For her to ask where to put a dirty dish was simply unacceptable.

"Over there," she answered after pointing at a sink with soapy water.

Georgianne placed the dish and returned to her phone. Her mind was somewhere else. As if she had forgotten where she stood, she lingered for a few minutes next to her mother, scrolling absentmindedly. Agnus reached for the dirty dish and bumped into her daughter.

"Georgianne," she stated.

"Hmm?"

"Georgianne!"

"What?"

"Do you need something?"

Georgianne looked up and scanned the kitchen. "I am sorry, mom. I am trying to look at something."

"What are you looking for?"

Georgianne lifted her phone. "I'm looking at master's programs."

Agnus attention was peaked. They had briefly discussed her daughter's continued education in the past, but it was never really a topic Georgianne entertained. Now that she was taking the initiative, Agnus wanted to investigate.

"Why are you looking at programs?"

"Just interested."

Georgianne moved towards the kitchen counter and sat on the bar stool. Agnus wiped her hands free of suds and turned towards her daughter. She leaned on the counter and rested her upper body on her folded arms.

"You haven't really been interested so far. What's changed your mind?"

"Allison," Georgianne explained as she put her phone, face down, on the counter. "Ever since she enrolled in seminary, I've been giving my own masters a thought. Figured it would be nice to get now while I'm young. At least before Michael and I get married."

The skin above Agnus' eyelids tightened as her eyes widened. *Allison? Seminary?* How on Earth could her sister afford that? Surely, Allison wasn't paying for it. Was this really what Arlene was spending her inheritance on?

Typical, Agnus thought to herself. *She gets a check for a little more than $300k, and now she blows a bunch of it on a master's degree for her confused daughter? And seminary? Really?*

"What is Allison studying?"

"She told me it's a degree in missions work. I can't remember the name."

"Which college?" Agnus pressed.

"Rochester."

Agnus turned and grabbed her phone quickly from beside the sink. A few tabs later, she pulled up a web page that broke down the average tuition for the University of Rochester.

$80,000.

Agnus's eyes narrowed. Here, her sister is dying, unable to pay for her own medical care, and her selfish niece is about to take her for more than a third of her net worth. Why? Just so she can preach to poor people across the seas. *Ridiculous.*

"Well," she began, clicking her phone off and putting it back on the counter. "Choose wisely, Georgianne. Your father and I will only put our money towards something that matters."

Georgianne swallowed a sarcastic comment and grabbed her phone again. With a small shove, she pushed the bar stool back and retreated to her bedroom. It was an expected response from her mother. She wasn't surprised.

As her daughter disappeared, Agnus kept her back towards her, continuing with the dishes in the sink. Her mind had cleared more than before, and her filing system was starting to snap back into place. Now, the thoughts she brought to center attention were on her own finances. The nearly $1 million she had received. This time tomorrow, Harold would be taking $250,000 and investing in the new venture he had set up. It had always been the plan. Once Phyllis was gone, the additional proceeds were to be doubled and tripled in a surefire investment. In just a few short weeks, Agnus would be a millionaire. A goal would be met. It had taken a while, but everything finally fell into place.

She sighed deeply. The order had been restored.

She placed her daughter's now clean dish on the drying rack and carefully folded the towel next to the sink. She watched as the water drained, forming a small tunnel above the opening at the bottom. Immediately, she filed away her thought of riches and pulled another idea front and center.

Detective Thomas.

Earlier that day, the station had called her cell and requested a meeting at his office the following morning. When she asked what it was for, they simply said it was a follow-up of her mother's case. This confused Agnus. The case had been closed for some time now. The autopsy confirmed the overdose in her mother's blood system, which was consistent with the pill bottle that she had shown the detective. The living room was neat and orderly, and there were no signs of struggle.

So, why the follow-up? Had something been missed? Was there new evidence?

Impossible, she thought. There was nothing else.

She steadied her heartbeat. It was elevated. She hated surprises. She hated deviations even more. Plans were meant to be followed, and anything contrary to what was expected was a nuisance for Agnus.

She sighed deeply and flushed the frustration out like a draining sink. The nervousness and impatience seemed to tunnel in her stomach before disappearing completely. All she was left with was her normal resolve.

Quietly she cleared her throat and left to get ready for the evening. Detective Thomas and his questions would have to wait for her attention until the morning.

Chapter 14

Edgar started his day a couple of hours earlier than normal. Agnus Palmitieri, the daughter of P. Moore, his latest case's victim, would be waiting on him for his 9:00. He was sure of it. The past month, she was always a few minutes early to each meeting he called. It was as if she was more eager to close the case than he was. That was understandable, though. Most family members of the deceased would rather bury their dead and move on than drag out investigations for longer than needed.

It was that very reason that made Arlene, the other daughter's request to reopen the investigation more confusing. Everything had pointed to open and shut. Now, Arlene's concern over potential foul play cast a shade of doubt on everything Edgar had done so far. He didn't like that. It wasn't how he conducted his investigations.

He pulled his cruiser into the parking space in front of the retirement home. A quick elevator ride up to the third floor was met with an empty hallway. By this time, the yellow caution tape had been removed from Phyllis' apartment door. Everything seemed normal. If he hadn't been assigned the case, he would have never known a person had fallen to their death just weeks before. It was always a strange feeling to watch the world carry on so quickly after tragedy. It was as if it simply made more room for more tragic events to happen.

Edgar stood in the middle of the hallway and scanned the walls. His gaze settled on the lone camera that was nestled in the corner near the ceiling. He recalled the conversation he had with building security at the onset of the investigation. They told him the cameras had stopped working suddenly the day before the victim died. It was a strange coincidence, but there was nothing else that seemed to add anything of value, so he couldn't make anything of it at the time. When he viewed the footage from the day before, all he saw were residents, the occasional worker, and a handful of visitors—none of which had stopped at Phyllis' apartment door.

Slowly, he walked to the camera. Behind him, the elevator bell gave a small whine, and he heard the door slide open. He turned to find an elderly woman with a walker slowly shuffling to her apartment three doors down from Phyllis'. When she finally arrived, she put the key in the door and opened it. A small whistle noise emanated from her door and echoed down the hall towards Edgar. He tilted his head. It didn't sound like a real whistle. Instead, it was more like a machine. He thought it was odd.

He walked toward the woman's apartment. As he approached the door, the same whistle sound called out. Quickly, he followed the noise with his eyes and realized it was coming from a small camera doorbell next to the door frame. Edgar leaned in and observed. The circular camera lens adjusted slightly as his image grew larger in its reflection. After an idea struck him, he stood up and walked back in the direction he had come from. When he was far out of view, he turned and walked towards the door again. Sure enough, as soon as he appeared in the camera's view, the whistle noise called out, and a soft blue ring slowly formed around the camera lens. It was filming Edgar. The doorbell camera had automatically captured his presence in the hall.

Detective Thomas backed up and scanned the hallway. Out of all the doors, he counted four that had similar cameras. They were scattered just enough to potentially capture each angle of the hall near Phyllis' apartment. His heart quickened. It was a lead. He had missed the feeling of a true lead. With a flip of his wrist, he retrieved his cell and dialed his office.

"This is Thomas. We need to file a warrant on the P. Moore case. Tell the judge I need doorbell camera footage from all apartments on her floor from the night of her death."

The phone clicked off, and he turned back towards the elevator. With that in motion, it was time to meet Agnus at his office.

Agnus clutched her handbag tightly as she sat in the dingy waiting room at the front desk. Up to this point, the detective had always been in his office when she arrived, albeit early. But today, he was "on his way," according to the secretary. This frustrated Agnus. She simply couldn't understand why some people weren't able to keep their appointments straight. It was simple to her. Write it down, arrive early, and give yourself time to avoid any interruptions. After all, Agnus had things to do today, and this meeting was last minute.

The front door swung open abruptly, and Detective Thomas rushed through as if running from the sunlight outside. Immediately, he saw Agnus in one of the plastic chairs and straightened.

"Hello Mrs. Palmitieri. Thank you for your patience. If you'll follow me, we will talk in my office."

Agnus stood up and aggressively brushed any funk from the waiting room off her trousers. She followed the detective down the hall and to his office door, where he unlocked it and opened it wide. Once seated, Detective Thomas began.

"Would you like a coffee?"

"No, thank you. What is this meeting about?"

Straight to business. *Typical for this woman,* thought Edgar.

"Right. Thank you for meeting me on short notice, Ms. Palmitieri. I had just a couple of follow-up questions from your mother's investigation and wanted to bring you here to discuss. Due to the sensitive nature of her passing, I did not want to speak over the phone. I figured in person would be more appropriate."

"*Investigation?*" The word was punched rather than spoken. "I thought my mother's case was closed. She committed suicide. Why would there be an investigation?"

"Well, we hadn't quite closed your mother's case just yet. There were still a few papers to finish up. But as I looked over the findings, there was something that stuck out to me. I wanted to see if you could add more clarity."

Agnus's eyebrows did all the talking for her. She waited impatiently for the detective's questions.

With the file in hand, Edgar turned a few pages and read from the folder.

"On the night of your mother's death, the investigators found an empty teacup in the sink. You had mentioned that you served your mother tea with her medicine every evening. Is that correct?"

"That's correct."

"And the night of her death, you had served her that tea before you left, correct?"

"Correct."

"What time in the evening did your mother typically take her medicine?"

Agnus shifted slightly. "Do you mean that night?"

"Any night. You said that she took it each evening. What time would you say she normally took it?"

Agnus thought for a brief moment before answering. "Well, the medication had some pretty heavy side effects, so I would give it to her right before bed so she could sleep it off. So, maybe eight on a normal night?"

Edgar turned a few more pages in the file. Pulling out a printed document, he continued.

"Right, the *Levodopa*, correct?"

"Correct."

"Says here that the normal side effects were lightheadedness, nausea, and confusion. And in some rare cases, hallucinations. Is that right?"

"That's right."

"You had told the investigators that your mother typically suffered from all the side effects each time she took it. Especially the confusion and hallucinations. Is this why you would normally give it to her around 8 in the evening?"

"That's correct. Normally, she would head to bed shortly afterward and fall asleep. That way, she wouldn't have to deal with the issues."

"Is that what happened the night she died?"

"What?"

"Did you give your mother the *Levodopa* at eight, and she went to bed?"

Silence. Agnus paused for a moment. *What was the investigator going on about? What had she missed?*

"Well, I think it was a tad earlier than normal that evening. I believe I had a prior engagement I had to get to, and we both agreed for her to take her pill a couple of hours earlier than normal so I could help her to bed."

"What time would you say she took it?" Edgar asked. He placed the paperwork on his desk and leaned in slightly.

"I have no clue," Agnus explained. "Maybe 6?"

Silence. Edgar leaned back and crossed his arms. Agnus squinted her eyes slightly, trying to read his face.

"I'm sorry," she interjected. "What are you getting at here?"

Edgar shook his head dramatically. "I'm just trying to get a solid timeline. That's all. Our office got the call about your mother's body on the side of the street at 9:14 that evening. If you gave her the meds at 6 pm like you are telling me, and she then promptly went to bed like she normally did, then by the time she would have fallen to her death, she would have been sleeping close to three hours."

"And?" Agnus made sure her question sounded angry.

"And, Mrs. Palmitieri, there have been no reported examples of your mother getting up randomly throughout the night and hallucinating. In fact, the examples you and your sister shared with our investigators explained that her moments of confusion in the past always happened during the day. Is that correct?"

"Yes, it's correct that her past moments of *crazy delusion* happened during the day. Why would that make any difference in what she did to herself that night? Maybe she got up to use the restroom. Maybe a noise woke her up. Why would that have anything to do with me?"

Detective Thomas ignored the last question. "According to your conversation at the scene of her death, you would crush up her pills and mix them with her tea, correct?"

"Yes..."

"Why is that?"

"Because she was in her eighties. Taking a pill had become a struggle. I figured crushing them up and mixing them with tea was easier."

"I see," Edgar responded. "Of course, the problem with that is there would be no clear way to prove that the right dosage was given, right?"

Agnus stood up abruptly. The chair she sat on flew backward and nearly slammed against Edgar's door.

"Are you suggesting that I gave my mother too many pills? Do you honestly think I killed my own mother?"

Edgar leaned back and crossed his arms once again. "I never said that, Ms. Palmitieri. I'm simply asking if it would be possible that when serving your mother her evening tea, you had mistakenly crushed up more than her normal dosage of *levodopa* for that evening."

"No! It's not possible!" Agnus screamed. "I took care of my sick and dying mother for years on my own. And in that time, I never mixed up, added to, or forgot her medication. I am a woman of intelligence and order. My ducks are always in a row. To think that you would ever accuse me of intentionally harming or even accidentally harming my own mother is ridiculous. I should talk to your supervisor!"

"Mrs. Palmitieri, please know that no one here thinks you meant to harm your mother. I applaud you for taking care of her as long as you have. I am simply trying to determine why a god-fearing woman like your mother would have decided to get up after a deep sleep and randomly take a handful of her medication that she knew would throw her into a deluded panic. It just doesn't add up."

"Well, Detective Thomas," she hissed. "That's not my problem. Now, if you'll excuse me, I have an appointment across town that I would very much like to not be late for. Anything else you would like to ask me, you can do so with my lawyer present."

Agnus snatched her handbag from the floor next to her chair and threw the strap over her shoulder. Edgar pushed his chair back and, after closing the file and picking up the folder, stood up and walked towards the door of his office.

"I understand. The good news is we have evidence of the cup's original condition. I'm having a forensics swab for an exact measurement of the levodopa that was served to your mother that night. It'll help us in narrowing down how much she had in her system before she woke up and finished the job."

Agnus' eyes widened as her spine stiffened. Detective Thomas rounded his desk and opened the door.

"Thankfully, you were in such a hurry that you didn't clean the cup that evening."

With a wave of his hand, he ushered Agnus back out into the hall.

As she walked towards the front desk, he called after her, "We will let you know the results, Mrs. Palmitieri. Thank you again for your time!"

Agnus refused to look back or offer a response. Instead, she clutched her bag tighter as she rounded the corner, not breaking her aggressive stride at all. With a quick whoosh, she exited the building and made her way to her car. The morning sun was beaming brightly, and the reflection from the station's windows nearly blinded her as she threw her purse into the passenger side chair and slammed the car door shut. The heat that bounced off the building warmed her far more than she was comfortable with. It felt as if she was on fire.

Her heart was racing, and her throat was dry. Like most people who strived for successful lives, she had never been treated like a suspect in a criminal case before. Nor had she ever wanted to know the feeling. But now she did, and it was terrible. From this point forward, her goal was to get her name removed from Detective Thomas' list.

And the best way to do that, she thought, *was to replace it with someone else's.*

Chapter 15

Arlene sat nervously in the doctor's office. Her cane leaned against the expensive mahogany desk in front of her. In her lap was a cashier's check in a bank envelope. She gripped it tightly but was careful not to cause any creases. She had never seen that much money at once. Inside the envelope, the check read in bold blue letters:

$275,000

Even the paper felt heavy. She might as well have been holding the full amount in dollar bills. As she handed the check over to her right hand, she jaggedly rubbed her tremoring left hand on her pant leg to dry off the sweat that had accumulated. She wanted to make sure the check and envelope would not get wet. She was not sure the bank would cut her a new one.

Above the empty leather desk chair, a large diploma was encased behind glass and framed with a golden, ornate square. In dark green letters, the words read:

Katherine Arden, MD

Doctorate in Neurosurgery

Everything Arlene had read confirmed to her that Dr. Arden was the greatest neurosurgeon in the field of Amyotrophic Lateral Sclerosis disease and treatment. After finally getting in for her first meeting, Dr. Arden shared the exciting news about a new procedure that was supposed to delay the symptoms of her ALS significantly, potentially giving her 5-10 more good years before her body succumbed. It was highly experimental and contained a lot of unknowns, but it was hope in an otherwise dismally unhopeful situation.

The only catch is the price. Because of the risk and intensity of the procedure—essentially invasive spinal and brain surgery—the cost was astronomical. Not to mention the follow-up care and perpetual medication that followed. Only a small population of patients nationwide have undergone the procedure up to this point, with the bulk of them having done it right here in this office by none other than Dr. Arden.

It took every ounce of strength in Arlene's emotions to keep the tears from reflowing. She had already spent her morning crying. A week ago, there would have been no way Arlene could have agreed to the surgery. Insurance companies did not cover it due to the risks and the fact that it was "voluntary." Therefore, if you did not have the means, you had no chance to become a candidate. But thanks to Phyllis and her husband, Arlene was more than able.

The door opened behind her, somewhat startling Arlene. A thin, blonde woman appeared with a white coat. She had small diamond studs in her ears and her hair was pulled up fashionably into a messy bun, held together by a pencil. She was beautiful with kind eyes and a warm smile.

"Hello, Arlene!"

"Hello, Dr. Arden."

"How are we feeling today?"

"Today has been a good day so far. I had a couple of stumbles in the morning, but they were tame compared to what they could be."

"That's great to hear."

The doctor turned towards her filing cabinet and opened a drawer. After a quick look, she retrieved a file and returned her attention to her patient.

"So, I have good news. We have an opening for your surgery at the end of this month. It would fall on a Tuesday. Would that work?"

Arlene smiled nervously. "Yes, Tuesday works. At this point, any day would work!"

"Great! The surgery should take approximately six hours, including pre-op and post-op. We would want to keep you in the hospital for at least three days following the procedure to keep an eye on you. As long as everything goes according to plan, we should see improvement in your mobility before discharging you from the hospital."

Arlene nodded and continued smiling. *Improved mobility.* It was a phrase she thought she'd never hear again. Everything since her diagnosis was rooted in failure. Failure to stand without assistance. Failure to control certain movements. Failure to see a bright future. To now hear the chance of improvement was like a cold glass of water in an empty desert.

"Now, from what I can see, the only thing that remains to get you scheduled is the payment," Dr. Arden continued. "Are you aware of the balance?"

"They told me last week when we first met. I believe it was $275,000?"

"Yes, that's the payment estimate for the surgery, including an estimate for anesthesia. It's subject to change, pending your stay in the hospital afterward. We hope your insurance will cover your admission, but we can't be certain. Now, we would only expect you to put 10 percent down to secure your date. Most patients will pay in payments after the surgery. Have they discussed your options?"

"They have, but it's okay," Arlene responded. She lifted the envelope and placed it on the doctor's desk. "I have a cashier's check here for the full amount."

Dr. Arden's eyes bulged. Arlene could tell this surprised her.

"Oh wow!" she remarked. "Well, I'll have you leave that with the ladies at the front desk when you leave today. That definitely makes things easier."

Arlene nodded quietly. She wasn't sure how to respond. A part of her wanted to explain that this wasn't her money. It was a gift from her parents. Deep down, she felt as if she wasn't worthy of such an amount. It was like she had stolen it somehow.

But she knew it wasn't true. This money was a blessing.

In the back of her mind, she heard her mother's voice whisper, *Remember, my love. He knows the plans He has for us. Plans to prosper and not harm. Plans for hope and a future.*

It was her mother's favorite scripture. She felt the same threat of tears choke in her throat. Once again, she forced it down.

The two women shook hands, and Dr. Arden escorted Arlene out the door and towards the front desk. Like the doctor, the two ladies who sat at the desk were surprised to see a check for more than a quarter million dollars. Arlene did what she could to hide her embarrassment and fervently thanked the whole office for her opportunity. She saw them as angels, sent by God to remind her that He had not forgotten her.

///

Later that same evening, Agnus finally made it home. Her husband, Harold, had already gotten home. She could tell by the pearl-white Escalade that sat in the driveway. She hated that car. She felt her husband could show his wealth more prudently if he'd purchased a smaller SUV. Maybe a Jaguar or a Porsche. Instead, he drove around a tank with more chrome on the bumper than any she had ever seen.

"It's a gaudy-looking thing," she had once told him. It hurt his feelings; she could tell. But it didn't matter. Sooner or later, she hoped he'd trade it in, and then she would be proud to see him scoot all over town.

Once inside, Agnus threw her purse on the counter with a loud thud and tossed the keys next to the light switch. Harold had just poured himself a glass of red wine when he looked up in concern at his frustrated wife.

"Everything okay?" he asked.

"No," Agnus answered sharply. She went straight to the sink and plugged up the drain. There were two forks that her husband had just thrown in there. Enough to give her an excuse to clean.

Harold sat his wine glass back down and made his way over to his wife.

"How did the meeting go with Detective Thomas?"

"Terrible," Agnus explained. "He all but accused me of poisoning mom the night she died."

"What?" replied Harold. His mouth stayed open in surprise.

"Yep," continued Agnus. "And apparently, they are running tests on the dirty cup that mom drank from before she went to bed that evening."

Agnus reached for the sponge and squirted a small drop of blue dish detergent on it. Before she could reach down and grab one of the forks, Harold stopped her and removed the sponge from her hand, tossing it into the sink. He then grabbed both her shoulders and turned her to face him. His expression was a mixture of shock and horror.

"What do you mean they are running tests on the dirty cup? *What dirty cup?*"

Agnus lifted her chin in defiance. "The dirty cup that was left in mom's sink the night she died. I had forgotten to clean it after serving her tea."

The silence was so loud that all the other noises couldn't be heard. Tension flooded the kitchen. Harold slowly let go of his wife's shoulders and backed away, still locked in a horrific gaze.

"Aggie, that means."

"I know what that means, Harold!" Agnus shouted. She turned again to the sink and picked the sponge back up. After a quick moment, she flung it against the window above her head and let out a sharp scream.

Right on cue, Georgianne entered the kitchen behind her parents. Her face was puzzled.

"Mom?" she asked carefully, looking between both her parents. "Is everything okay?"

Agnus popped tall immediately and collected herself. After a quick brush of her blouse, she turned to face her daughter with an almost unnatural grin on her face.

"Yes, dear," she explained. "Everything is fine. Are you off to see Allison?"

Still concerned, Georgianne responded, "Yeah. She and Aunt Arlene are cooking dinner tonight, so you do not have to cook for me. Also, Michael just arrived. He said he was going to use the restroom and then leave right after me. He parked out back near my room."

Agnus shot a quick glance at her husband, who kept his head down.

"Sounds great, dear. Be safe, and let me know when you get there."

Georgianne nodded and disappeared out the door, closing it behind her. Once the coast was clear, Harold lifted his gaze back to his wife. Just then, Michael appeared in the kitchen hallway. His face was as white as a ghost, and he had lost weight. Agnus scanned both the men with a sharp expression and then shook her head.

"Listen, boys. I am going to need both of you to man up and get with the story here. I have worked far too hard to get to this point, and I have no use for two men who cannot pick their heads up and move forward." Her eyes bore a hole into her future son-in-law's face. "You need to shape up. What have you told Georgianne?"

"Nothing. I have told her nothing."

"Keep it that way," she continued. Then she looked over at Harold. "And you, where are we at with the investment?"

Harold cleared his throat and lifted his chin. "The money has been sent. The broker assured me we would see a return within a week and a half. Once the company goes public, we should see at least a 500-percent gain on the investment made. That should grow by another 350 percent by year's end. This will put the full value at around $5 million when it is all said and done."

"Good," Agnus responded. "Until then, we need to beat this Detective Thomas to the reason behind my mother's death. Right now, he is sniffing around the idea that I may have accidentally put too much of Mom's medicine in her tea. I do not want my name anywhere close to a cause of death for that woman. Do you understand me?"

The last comment was directed solely at Michael, whose already pale face turned even more shades whiter.

"Ms. Agnus, I don't know if I—"

"Shut up, Michael," Agnus snarled as she walked closer to him. "You listen to me. I know exactly who you are and what you've done. Don't think for one second, I won't tell the world if it means protecting my own self." She pointed at Harold. "Or my family."

Michael nodded slowly. Harold gritted his teeth and stepped between the scared young professional and his ravenous wife.

"Agnus, listen," he began. "I think I may have an idea."

Agnus quickly made eye contact with her husband. She didn't say a word.

Harold continued, "I was doing a routine inventory of upcoming surgeries at the hospital. It's a part of a monthly earnings report I put together for the trustees. When I got the report for this past week, I saw something very interesting."

"Spit it out, Harold," Agnus retorted. "What did you find?"

Harold paused. Deep down inside him, he worried about the information he was about to share. He loved his wife, but the reality was she was a scary woman. And with the right weapon, he was fully convinced she was capable of terrible damage. After a quick shuffle of his feet, he swallowed hard and complied.

"Your sister," he started. "She is scheduled for surgery at the end of the month."

"Okay?" Agnus responded. "What does that have to do with *anything* we are talking about?"

Harold continued. "The surgery she is having is one of the most expensive our neurosurgery department offers, to the tune of about $300,000. From what I understand, it's elective and, therefore, not normally covered by most insurance. This means the normal patient would have to pay for this out of pocket."

Agnus leaned back. Without realizing it, she grabbed her husband's wine glass and took a sip. Harold was fine with it. Whatever it took to calm her down.

"Apparently," he continued. "Arlene turned in a cashier's check today worth $275,000. Of course, this was enough of an anomaly to make my report."

Agnus leaned against the countertop. Her mind was doing somersaults.

"How can this help us, Harold? We all know she just received $375,000 from our mother's inheritance. That would make sense."

"Right," Harold explained. "And it also makes sense that a daughter, desperate for a chance to live long enough to see her child graduate college, would do *whatever* it takes to pay for the surgery that would get her there."

The revelation hit Michael square between the eyes. A flash of color reentered his cheeks.

"Motive!" he shouted.

Agnus shot a glance at Michael, sharp enough to stick in the wall behind him. Michael immediately swallowed the rest of his sentence. After another sip, she tilted her head.

"So, we could tell the detective that we worry my sister killed my mother in order to receive her inheritance so that she could pay for her ALS surgery. That may just work."

Harold nodded his head. Beneath his stoic expression, however, his breath wavered. It was evil. But it *could* work.

"Harold, see if you can get something to prove the charge. We can show that to the detective tomorrow. And you," Agnus looked at Michael. "You need to distract Georgianne. She's been spending a lot of time with Arlene and Allison. I don't want her to get caught up in this."

After a couple of nods of agreement, the two men parted ways, Harold to his study and Michael out the same door his fiancé had exited moments earlier. Agnus was left alone in her domain, swirling the remaining sip of wine around the bottom of the stemware. She watched as the dark red liquid stained the glass, then cleared instantly as it drained to the other side. The plan could work. It was a long shot, but at this point, anything was a guess. Why not let the detective guess about her sister?

She took the final sip and swallowed. As she carefully placed the glass back in the sink, a thought stopped her in her tracks. Her brothers and sister all received $375,000 from her mother's passing. Arlene was spending $275,000 on the surgery, as well as signing up her daughter for a 2-year program with a tuition cost of more than $80,000 per year. That means there was more money spent than what her otherwise destitute sister would have. The math didn't add up. Somewhere, Arlene was hoarding $60,000.

Agnus scoffed out loud. There's no way Arlene had that type of money lying around.

Unless? No. There was nothing else in her parents' estate. Any extra money was funneled through the sale of the home and directly into Agnus' account. She was sure of it.

The thought nagged at her still. She couldn't stomach the thought of leaving money on the table, of anything extra given to her sister who, for years now, was incapable of doing anything good for anybody.

She would have to investigate it further, if anything, to distract herself from the nonsense happening with the detective.

There were so many thoughts, so many ideas. Agnus shook her head quickly. Like perfect little soldiers, all the different thoughts fell into line and returned to their categories.

One thing at a time, Agnus, she muttered under her breath. *One thing at a time.*

Chapter 16

The phone clicked as Detective Thomas returned the receiver to its base. His mind was buzzing. Unconsciously, he rubbed his temples as he pondered the odd conversation. Just then, Harold, the decedent's son-in-law, husband to Agnus—a primary suspect at the moment—had called to inform him of some damaging evidence.

Quickly, his thoughts traced back to his days in narcotics. He remembered his old Major explaining the number one rule of solving major crimes: follow the money. It never failed. Where there were large purchases, clear motivation, or outright financial need, there was always a tie back to the suspect.

Now, while he slowly worked his way through hours of doorbell camera footage from the days leading up to the death of Phyllis Moore, a potential smoking gun had been hand-delivered by a concerned relative.

But the potential aggressor was what concerned Edgar the most: Arlene.

Just a few days prior, Arlene had secured a major elective surgery for her condition that could have only been made possible with the inheritance provided *after the death of her mother.*

Edgar had always made it a point to avoid becoming emotionally invested in any person, whether a suspect or victim, during an open investigation. It made it easier to separate personal bias from the twists and turns of a crime case. But he would be lying to himself if this particular revelation didn't sting him more than usual. After all, Arlene had sat in his office, made a plea to reinvestigate, and seemed incredibly saddened by her mother's passing.

But the evidence was too obvious not to follow up. He braced himself before picking back up the phone.

"Dial Arlene Sky, please."

"Yes sir," the voice on the other end responded.

After a few rings, the phone picked up, and Arlene's voice came through.

"Detective Thomas?"

"Hi, Arlene," Edgar started. "How are you doing?"

"I'm fine, thank you. Did you find something out?"

Her eagerness made this conversation even harder.

"Arlene, some new evidence has been brought to my attention. Are you available to swing by the station this afternoon? I'd like to ask you a few more questions."

"I'm actually having dinner with my daughter and niece this evening, but we should be finished around 8. If you don't have any plans, I could put on a pot of coffee, and you could come by. My driving options become very limited the later it gets. Ubers don't normally drive this far out of town after rush hour."

Edgar smiled slightly, then cleared his throat.

"That would be fine. I'll see you at 8."

When the call ended, he sighed deeply. He was still struggling with the potential of this lead. Arlene had proven to be compliant, sincere, and, for all he knew, a wonderful daughter.

But if his years in the force had taught him anything, the most likely suspects are the ones you least expect. He would be armed and ready despite his reservations.

The knock on the door startled Arlene, even though she had prepared for this visit all afternoon. The sound of small conversations and clinking plates and cups being washed in the sink carried on from the kitchen as Georgianne and Allison cleared the table and cleaned up after dinner.

"Mom, do you need me to get that?"

"You're fine, darling. I can manage."

Arlene leaned against her cane and shuffled towards the front door. She opened it wide and greeted the detective as he smiled a brief smile in response.

"Hello, Ms. Sky."

"Please, detective. Call me Arlene. Come on in."

The detective entered and looked around.

Arlene made her way back to her chair. "I hope you don't mind; my daughter and niece are still cleaning up after dinner. As far as I'm concerned, they are welcome to listen to whatever you have to say. I know they are just as concerned as I am that this case is resolved. Would you like a cup of coffee?"

"That would be fine. Thank you."

Just then, Georgianne entered and greeted the detective with a smile and handshake. "Hello, Detective Thomas. I'm Georgianne, Arlene's niece."

"Is your mother…"

"Agnus," Georgianne finished. "Don't hold that against me." She chuckled softly.

"Georgianne!" Arlene retorted. It was a playful rebuke.

"I'm just kidding, Aunt Arlene," Georgianne assured. "I just know the hoops she's probably putting this poor man through." She turned to face the detective again. "My mother has a knack for being…thorough."

Edgar smiled. "That's a good way to put it."

Behind Georgianne, Allison appeared with a cup of coffee in hand.

"I wasn't sure how you liked it, Detective. I can grab some creamer if you'd like."

"Black is fine," explained Edgar. "Thank you."

The two young women found a spot on the couch near Arlene. All three ladies stared patiently at the detective. That sense of discomfort returned in full force. Obviously, he can't force them not to be there, but if he were to accuse Arlene of potential murder, it might be best if her daughter and niece weren't there to bear witness.

He took a small sip of the coffee and cleared his throat before placing it on a nearby table.

"Arlene, are you sure you wouldn't want to speak more privately?"

"Detective, my family is the closest thing I have to me. We all loved my mother dearly. Anything you need to tell me, you can say to them as well. We are all equally invested."

"Understood," Edgar responded. "Well, I'll cut to the chase here. I received an interesting phone call from your brother-in-law, Harold, this morning. He told me that you had recently made a considerable down payment at the hospital for surgery at the end of this month. Something to the tune of $ 300k?"

Silence. The air in the living room tightened as if it was wound closely around a spool. Edgar scanned Arlene's face quickly for any tell-tale signs of regret or confession. All he saw was surprise.

"How did he...," began Arlene. Then, the color flushed from her face. Edgar couldn't help but take in an obvious sign of realization.

"The hospital," she finished. "He found out through the hospital."

Edgar leaned back quickly. He hadn't expected that response.

"What do you mean 'the hospital?'" he responded.

"Harold must have found out about the surgery through the hospital. He works there."

"He's the CEO," explained Georgianne.

"Mom, what surgery?" interjected Allison.

Silence again.

"I didn't want to tell you this way, Allison," responded Arlene. "I wanted to wait until we got closer to the date. It was a surprise..."

Another realization slammed against Edgar's countenance.

"Wait a minute," he interrupted. "Arlene, are you saying you didn't tell your daughter about your surgery."

Arlene shook her head softly. "I did not tell anyone. Not yet."

Edgar leaned back completely in the chair. His mind was buzzing again.

"So, Harold did not know you were having the surgery? He found out through hospital records?"

Out of the corner of his eye, he saw Arlene's niece's countenance go from surprise to a darker shade of irritability. He was not sure, but it was almost as if she had her own realization. After all, there was a lot of that going around this evening.

"Mom, what kind of surgery is this? Why didn't you tell me?" continued Allison.

"It's a breakthrough treatment," explained Arlene. "I had planned to tell you right before I had it and then surprise you with the results. My doctor says if everything goes according to plan, I should get a lot more of my mobility back. I may even be able to get my license back next year."

"Are you serious?" Allison responded. Tears formed in her eyes.

"Yes," responded Arlene. "I wanted to surprise you by driving to your graduation next year."

It was a warm moment. Edgar couldn't deny it. But it didn't answer any of his questions. He had to interrupt the conversation again.

"I'm sorry, Arlene. I have to ask. Why now? Why would you suddenly choose to do such an expensive, important surgery? What changed?"

It was an obvious question with an obvious answer, but Edgar wanted to hear it for himself. This could be the turning point in this investigation. Whether he liked it or not, Arlene's response could finally reveal her motivation.

After a pause, Arlene grabbed her cane and slowly stood up. With a brief shuffle, she walked towards her kitchen counter and retrieved an old, worn bible. With her right hand, still leaning on the cane, she opened it up and pulled out a letter. She made her way slowly over to the detective and handed it to him.

"This is from my mother, Detective," she explained. "It's in her own handwriting. You can read it. She gave this to me with a promise that my medical needs would be taken care of."

Edgar read the words carefully. Like rapid fire, details were clicking together. This was unrelated money from a secret trust that was only meant for Arlene. It was meant for her care. *Motive?*

Arlene turned her attention to her daughter and caught the detective's gaze. He wasn't sure, but it felt as if she could read his mind.

Arlene saw the question on Detective Thomas' face clearly. Like a clear window, she felt a sense of divine discernment fall over her. *He thinks I did it,* she thought.

At once, she fought off a whiff of anger. How could anyone think she would deliberately kill her mother so she could fund a surgery that only promised another decade or two? Arlene would have much rather spent whatever time she had left with her whole family alive and well than have to bury her mother.

But then, from the same discernment came a warm feeling of grace and understanding. This man was doing his job. That was it. It was up to Arlene to explain her side. The rest was in her Father's hands.

"Detective Thomas," she began. "I loved my mother more than anything. She taught me so much about this life: how to pray, how to serve my Heavenly Father, and how to raise my daughter in the footsteps of the Lord."

Arlene turned towards Allison, who was wiping away a fresh set of tears. She turned back to the detective and continued, "I did not kill my mother. I know you have to ask these questions, and you have to be suspicious. But from the bottom of my heart, I did not kill her. I read that letter you are holding for the first time after my mother was found dead. I had no clue I was getting that additional money until she was gone. I can't prove that, but it's the truth."

Detective Thomas folded the letter back up and placed it in its envelope. He looked at Arlene carefully.

"Who is Douglas Taylor?"

"He is a family friend. He was a lawyer, which Dad sometimes used when he first started his company."

"And he was the one who managed this trust?"

Arlene shrugged her shoulders. "I believe so. His name is on the paperwork. It did not make a lot of sense to me either, but when I asked him about it, he made it seem as if Mom and Dad did not want the money to be found out by Agnus. That is also why I've kept this quiet."

Detective Thomas breathed in deeply. He placed the envelope on the table next to his coffee cup and leaned forward.

"Arlene, I believe you," he responded. "But there is still something that doesn't make sense."

"What?" Arlene asked.

"Why would Harold go against every HIPPA law known to mankind and tell me this information?"

Before Arlene could respond, Georgianne stood up. Her hands were balled into fists, and she was shaking slightly.

"I don't know," she blurted. "But you bet I'm going to find out!"

Still deep in thought, Edgar turned his key inside the door handle of his cruiser and unlocked the car. Suddenly, he sensed something behind him in the dark night. With a quick turn, he backed against the car and spun around.

It was Allison, Arlene's daughter.

"I'm sorry!" she exclaimed. "I didn't mean to startle you."

"It's okay," he responded. "Occupational hazard."

Allison was quiet for a beat. Edgar leaned in and crossed his arms.

"Detective Thomas," she whispered. "I know you're just doing your job, but I feel like I need to tell you that I firmly believe my mother is innocent here."

Edgar nodded. He tried to come up with a way to tell her he wholeheartedly agreed, but he couldn't commit to it before there was proof. The words didn't form as he had hoped. Thankfully, Allison added more before he could respond.

"It's no secret that I've never been a fan of my aunt. She can be... cold-hearted at times. I'm not saying that I think she did anything, but I feel like you need to spend more time looking at her than my disabled mother. After all, she spent so much time over there."

"She explained that she was her primary caregiver for years."

"Years? Detective, my grandmother was only sick for a few short months."

Another domino falls. "Months?"

"Yeah," explained Allison. "My grandmother was perfectly fine until just a short while ago. Then, it seemed like Aunt Aggie was over there every day. Before you knew it, Aggie controlled everything: her meds, bills, and life. It was only then that she started to decline."

This was not completely new. Edgar knew that Phyllis had declined quickly, according to reports from the family. Even Agnus herself stated that her mother's decline was swift. What caught him off guard was the confusion around how long Agnus had spent her days at her mother's house before her death. According to Agnus, it was long enough to show confidence and care. But to Allison, it was only a short while. Just long enough for Agnus to step in and escalate things.

"I appreciate you telling me this," Edgar said finally. "It helps."

"I just want to protect my mother, Detective. She has been through so much, and I know she would never hurt her mother. I trust her."

It was the same expression he had heard from countless victims, families, and suspects over the years. Trust had become a funny word to him. It had lost its luster, frankly.

The door of his cruiser shut behind him. As he turned the key in the ignition, he thought about the conversations from the evening. So much to unpack. So much to consider.

As he turned down the road heading home, he could not help but think to himself, *maybe I should trust her, too.*

Chapter 17

"I didn't really know Phyllis very well," said Martha Anne, the tenant who lived a door to the right of the crime scene. "She had only been in the apartment for a few weeks. I talked with her a couple of times in the hallway, but that is really it."

Edgar scratched the notes on his pad. "Did you see anyone else visit Phyllis while she was here? Maybe someone in the evening?"

"I did see her daughter visit quite often. She was not a very talkative person, but she was over there faithfully every day. Then, of course, I saw her grandson visit in the evening."

"Grandson?" Edgar asked. To his knowledge, there were no grandsons locally.

"Well, I assumed it was her grandson," Martha Anne explained. "He was a tall-looking fellow. I only saw him a couple of times. I cannot remember when. He always wore black. I figured he was one of those goth people, but that is none of my business. The young folk can dress however they..."

Her voice continued quietly while Edgar mulled over the description. A tall-looking man, young, dressed in black. It was an odd image. For some reason, it felt like he had heard that description somewhere before.

Then it hit him. Quickly, he scoured back over the previous pages in his notepad. Turning abruptly, he searched for some of the previous notes he had taken. Scribbles about smaller cases passed him in a blur until he saw Phyllis' name appear towards the front of the pad. That is where he read it:

Hallucinations. A tall figure dressed in black. Stalking her. The daughter calls it fake.

It matched the description. But who was this? Obviously, if Martha Anne had seen it, then it was not fake. *Could this have been an aggressor? Was it possible that Phyllis had not killed herself?*

"Thank you for your time, ma'am," he interrupted the woman. "I think I have what I need."

The woman responded with a quick nod and smile, and Edgar raced back to his car before heading toward his office. Once he arrived, he closed the door behind him and pulled up the footage from the doorbell cameras. He had poured over them, searching for a familiar figure that could have been a suspect. To this point, he had only seen a few neighbors and the occasional staff member. Nothing out of the ordinary.

He pulled up the file for Martha Anne's apartment. Quickly, he pushed the mouse backward, tracking to an hour before the supposed time of death. With another click, the footage started up. For nearly 30 minutes, all he saw was a blank wall. No one and nothing came across the viewfinder.

Another 10 minutes went by, and still nothing. Edgar sighed deeply. He reached and grabbed the mouse to switch over to another camera view when something caught his eye. It wasn't a person but a small smudge-like shadow in the left corner. He paused the video. The shadow appeared and lingered for around 10 seconds before disappearing off-screen in the direction of what would have been Phyllis' apartment.

He backed up the film again. Once the shadow reappeared, he paused the video and dragged a square over the shadow. Then he pressed the plus sign. This blew the image up while also rendering it clearly. He clicked it two more times. After a brief moment, the video cleared, and he saw what looked like a shirt sleeve. It was black.

Edgar leaned towards his computer. His eyes scanned the shirt sleeve up and down. The black cloth clung to the arm as it traced down, ending just above the wrist. From what he could gather, whoever it was reached down to grab something from the ground, causing the arm to be slightly visible in the corner of this video. He zoomed in further. There was something on the wrist.

A fish. But it wasn't any old fish. Rather, this was one of those same fish that he had often seen on the bumpers of cars around town. A "Jesus' fish" is what he had always heard it called.

He scribbled down in his notebook. Though it wasn't a clear lead, the idea of a black-clad individual appearing in the same hallway as Phyllis' apartment just moments before her death was suspicious enough. But now, the hard part had begun.

How on Earth would Edgar find someone with a small wrist tattoo? Where would he start?

The grandson, he thought. Who was the grandson? That would be his first question. And he knew the right person to ask.

Chapter 18

Arlene answered the door. On the other side, her sister was standing impatiently.

"Hello, Aggie," she answered.

Agnus leaned in and offered her cheek for a quick peck.

"What are you up to today, Arlene?" she asked as she walked into her sister's home. It was a sharp, deliberate question—one she asked often when something was bothering her. She felt she already knew the answer. Normally, Arlene let it slide, but this time, it felt even more painful.

" I have plans to follow up with my doctor today," she answered quickly.

"Which doctor is this?" Agnus asked.

"It appears you may already know, Aggie."

Agnus turned abruptly; her eyes widened. She was not used to her sister being so brazen.

"I may have heard a rumor that you are having major surgery this month. Odd that you wouldn't let us know. After all, we are your family."

Arlene walked towards her chair. With her back turned, she visibly gritted her teeth, swallowing a harsh comeback. It took everything in her to keep her composure.

"Why are you here, Agnus?"

"I came to visit my sister," Agnus began. "And I wanted to ask you about something."

"Oh?"

"What are your plans for the money that Mom and Dad left you? I mean, the rest of it. After you finish paying for your surgery."

Arlene swallowed hard. Did she know about the additional money? Was this a way to entrap her? She had no clue where her sister was going with this.

Lord, give me wisdom, she thought.

"Well, the surgery is taking a big portion out of the inheritance Mom left us. And, of course, with Allison heading back to school, I plan to help pay her way there with whatever I have left."

"And how much is Allison's school?"

"Why are you asking?"

Agnus crossed her arms. "Arlene, it's no secret that you have not been the best of money managers. I just want to know how you plan to pay for everything you have committed to. The math simply doesn't add up."

"Well, Aggie," Arlene snarled. "I don't think that's any of your business."

"I was appointed executor of mom's estate. I knew every dime that went into your pocket, Arlene. You weren't given enough to pay for everything you are paying for."

"And?"

"And, if there was something else involving our parents' affairs that you knew and I didn't, I would call that a breach of their last wishes. I simply want to ensure the integrity of our parent's assets and make sure everything in our family is handled equitably."

Silence. The whole paragraph sounded rehearsed. Arlene was not sure, but she felt as if Agnus had prepared for this very conversation for some time.

"Aggie, I appreciate you swinging by and following up on our family's affairs. But I have plans. I'm going to ask you to leave now."

After a brief hesitation, Agnus stood up with her bag in hand and headed towards the door. Arlene made her way to the door as well and held it open for her sister. Before she walked out, Agnus turned abruptly and stood inches away from her sister's nose.

"Sis," she hissed with a wry smile. "One last thing."

"What's that?"

"I hope you know that these past few months, I have spent most of my waking hours taking care of our mother."

"Yes, I know, Agnus. And I'm very grateful—"

"That's not what I'm looking for. Arlene, I have spent most of my days helping her, feeding her, and even handling her affairs. And in that time, I have learned all the deep, dark corners of our mother's financial life. Understand that if there was anything that fell out of line, I would find it. And if I find out that anything may have led our mother to her grave early…," she paused and stared at her sister before continuing,"…I will make it my life's work to see that whoever was a part of it be buried beneath the jail. You have my word."

Arlene's heart beat faster than it had in a while. She was used to her sister's narcissistic behavior, but this was a first. It felt like a direct threat to her—an accusation.

"Agnus, I hope you don't think that—"

Agnus held up two fingers and placed them on her red lips. "Ah-ah-ah. Do not say anything else, Arlene. Just remember what I told you."

With that, she turned and walked to her car. The threat still hung in the air. Arlene watched as her sister turned back down the road and left her behind. Her blood boiled inside her body.

What are you up to, Agnus? she thought quietly. Who knew? But one thing was certain: Arlene had become a target. And the millions she received in secret started to feel like a cinderblock around her neck.

After closing the door and locking it, she retrieved her cell phone from her bag. Quickly, she found the name she was looking for and dialed it. The phone rang twice before a voice picked up on the other end.

"Hi, yes. This is Arlene Sky. Can I please speak with Mr. Taylor? Immediately."

Chapter 19

"Arlene, I need you to try and breathe through this. I can only imagine what you are going through."

The muted voice of Phyllis' kind daughter continued into his ear. Douglas instinctively grabbed his forehead with his index finger and thumb as if to stabilize himself—or keep the room from spinning. He had been in the family estate planning business for too long now. He was well aware of the impact that large sums of money had on a grieving family.

"The Detective reached out to me this morning. He's on his way to my office as we speak. I'll talk with him."

Another pause.

"You have my word, Arlene."

The phone clicked off right as his door opened. His secretary poked her head in briefly.

"Mr. Taylor, your 2:00 is here. Detective Thomas?"

"That's fine, Linda. Thank you."

The door swung wide, and the tired, slightly disheveled investigator stepped in past Linda. With a quick nod, the door shut behind him.

"Please, Detective, have a seat."

Detective Thomas scanned the room out of habit before finding the closest chair to Douglas' desk.

"Can I offer you something? Coffee or water?"

"No, thank you," he responded. "I appreciate you penciling me in on short notice."

"It's my pleasure. Anything for Phyllis' family."

Detective Thomas crossed his arms and stared momentarily at Douglas. It was slightly unnerving. Though Douglas was confident there was nothing that would pin him to this case other than his business dealings with Phyllis and her husband, for some strange reason, it felt as if he was a suspect in those few quick moments. Finally, Detective Thomas leaned forward and began.

"Mr. Taylor, the reason I'm here today is in reference to the estate that you worked on for Phyllis Moore and her husband quite a few years back. The one titled," he looked at the photocopy in his hand, "' Rock Construction Company Trust.'"

"Yes, I'm familiar."

"Can you tell me the thought process behind its creation? From what I've gathered, this was a separate trust tied to the business with only one beneficiary, correct?

"Yes, Arlene."

"Right," it was more of a question than a statement. Obviously, Detective Thomas wanted to know more about why that was the case.

"I've known the Moore family for years," Douglas explained. "I did a bunch of consulting work with Jacob when he first built his company back in the 70s. In 2015, I believe Jacob had a particularly strong year and approached me about estate planning. I, too, thought it was strange as I knew they had a family lawyer—Goldstein. He is a colleague I've known since pre-law. But they were adamant that they would keep this conversation between just the three of us. It was then that they had just found out about Arlene's diagnosis."

"The ALS, correct?"

"Correct," answered Douglas. "They were devastated. The goal was to take a considerable amount of the company's perceived value and place it into a trust. Their personal assets were to remain in the family estate under Goldstein, but the value of the company upon both Jacob and Phyllis' death was to directly go to the sole benefactor listed on the company's trust."

"Arlene."

"That's correct. They explained that it was a life insurance policy for their daughter. They knew that ALS had a terrible prognosis, and they wanted to make it so Arlene never had to worry about care, nurses, living conditions, or anything else that may come as a result."

"But why keep it a secret?" asked Detective Thomas.

"Agnus," was all Douglas responded.

The response was unnaturally quick. It was almost as if Douglas expected the Detective to know this already.

Maybe he did?

"Why Agnus?" asked the Detective.

Douglas drew in a deep sigh. "Listen, I'm not a counselor. I'm an estate planner and financial manager. I tend to stay away from family drama as much as possible. But it's impossible to not know how...," he struggled with the word, "difficult Agnus could be to her parents. From what Phyllis would describe after Jacob died, Agnus was incredibly deceptive. She tried to control everything when it came to her mother. From the house to the POA, to even her doctor's visits. Everything went through Agnus."

"Was that because of Phyllis' diminished capabilities?"

"What diminished capabilities?" asked Douglas, almost offended by the question. "Phyllis was one of the sharpest women I knew. That is why I have always considered her such a friend. Even when Jacob was alive, Phyllis managed the company's assets and books. She was highly intelligent and very frugal."

"But she was medicated with a highly powerful Parkinson's medication that most likely led to her untimely death. Wouldn't that mean her mental capabilities were diminished?"

Silence. Douglas felt himself swallow an entire paragraph. He did not want to be withholding, but he wasn't sure how much personal detail he should share. He squeezed his sweaty palms tightly and muttered a prayer under his breath.

Speak to me, Father. Tell me what I need to say.

"Mr. Taylor?" interrupted the Detective. "Is there something you need to tell me? I can only arrest what I know. Not what I don't."

An answer. Thank you, Father. Douglas let it rip.

"Detective, I knew my friend very well. She was an honest woman who placed herself behind her family and would never put them in any danger or difficulty if she could help it. I find it incredibly hard to believe that she would have kept a Parkinson's diagnosis a secret from her family. Let alone only trust that kind of information with Agnus."

"What are you saying?"

"I'm saying, Detective, I don't believe that Phyllis was sick. I believe she was taken advantage of."

The Detective's mouth dropped slightly. "By whom?"

"I'm not sure. But I refuse to believe that the woman I have worked with and known for all these decades chose to kill herself despite whatever mess her daughter was feeding her."

Detective Thomas leaned backward in the chair and crossed his arms, letting the words linger in the air for a brief moment. He could not be sure, but Douglas felt as if he saw a bit of relief in the Detective's face. Like a thought he had was just confirmed. But the man was a professional, and whatever Douglas thought he saw quickly vanished.

"Mr. Taylor, I appreciate your time. I'll get out of your hair."

Detective Thomas stood up and gathered his belongings, preparing to leave. Douglas was concerned that there was more to discuss. He felt he had done a disservice to the family. To Phyllis' memory. To Arlene and her innocence.

"Wait, Detective. One moment."

Detective Thomas paused and lowered his briefcase. He searched for something in Douglas' eyes. But all Douglas had to offer was concern.

"I don't want to outright accuse anyone. But I would be remiss if I did not say what I felt. Agnus had no business controlling what she did. Multiple times, Phyllis called me, concerned that her daughter was up to something. She only felt bad when Agnus was around."

Detective Thomas rubbed his chin with his thumb. Douglas added, "I don't know what that means, but I know it's not right. I'd start there."

Edgar and Mr. Taylor said their goodbyes, and the conversation was over. As Edgar drove out of the parking lot, his mind ran in circles. It seemed as if everything was pointing back to Agnus. The money, the motive, the control. It all seemed to make sense.

The only thing missing was the proof. As he turned down the main street, his phone rang. It was the station.

"This is Thomas."

"Tox reports came back from the cup in the P. Moore case."

"What does it say?"

"The dosage of Levodopa was highly elevated. At least three times what a typical dosage should be."

"What does forensics suggest?"

"They are saying it seems highly probable the dosage was intentional."

"Thanks."

The phone clicked through the dash. This was no surprise. Only more of a smoking gun. Now, the only missing piece was who added the medicine. Was it Agnus in her normal routine? Or was it Phyllis in an attempt to end it all?

More questions that needed more answers. But he was circling something significant. He could feel it.

Quickly, he pulled the car over into a nearby parking lot and retrieved his cell. Looking at his notebook, he dialed a number he had not used yet. The phone rang, and a voice picked up on the other end.

"Main Street Pharmacy, how can I help you?"

"Yes, this is Detective Thomas. Can I speak with the pharmacist, please? This is urgent."

Edgar waited patiently at the pharmacy counter. A quick observation showed that most of the techs were jumpy. It was obvious that the presence of an investigator at their store was not something they were used to.

After what felt like 15 minutes, a white-coat-clad pharmacist stepped forward from the back and smiled.

"Hey there, Detective."

"Dr. Andrews?" Edgar responded with an outstretched arm.

"Correct. Let's step over here, and we can talk privately."

The pharmacist was a handsome man, at least six feet tall, with a rather large paisley knot sticking out under his shirt collar beneath a buttoned lab coat. Edgar could tell he was well-paid and had been in the business for a while.

Dr. Andrews met Edgar over at a small consultation area. He remained on the pharmacy side of the half wall and beckoned the Detective to sit in a black customer chair opposite him. Edgar complied.

"What can I do for you, Detective?"

"Thanks for the time. Hopefully, I will be quick. I need to get some details about a pending investigation involving one of your patients. A Phyllis Moore."

The pharmacist turned towards a computer screen and typed into the keyboard. After a quick moment, he scanned what Edgar could only assume was a digital profile and then turned back towards him. That is when Edgar noticed a familiar tell-tale sign. Worry. The pharmacist's eyes widened slightly, and he did his best to conceal an obvious look of concern.

But nothing he did could stop the color draining from his face right before the Detective's eyes.

He cleared his throat and threw back a charming smile, "Ah yes, P. Moore. She has been a patient of ours for a long time. What can I help you with?"

"I understand that you've been giving her the drug Levodopa for the past few months. I was hoping to get a little more information on that. Maybe what orders were sent and from where."

"I'm sorry, Detective. As you know, our patients are protected by HIPPA, and I just can't..."

Edgar was prepared. He slid over a folded packet of white papers with a formal letterhead from a local judge.

"I have a warrant. Feel free to review." Edgar smelled blood.

The pharmacist stopped his explanation and stared at the folded papers on the counter. Without picking them up, he folded his arms and scratched the well-trimmed beard that was shaped under his chin.

"Understood. Well, Levodopa is a treatment for Parkinson's disease. Typically, it's administered in a powder form, but in some cases, it can be treated..."

Edgar held up a finger. "Let me stop you there, Dr. Andrews. I don't need a science lesson on what the drug is. I saw what it can do to a person. What I need is an understanding of where and how you came about the need to supply Ms. Moore with it."

Silence. The pharmacist's charisma and charm were failing. All that was left was an incredibly jumpy, nervous individual.

"Should I call my lawyer?"

"Why? Did you do something wrong?"

More silence. Finally, the pharmacist dropped the full charade and leaned in. "Listen, Detective, I don't want any problems here. I just filled out a prescription and gave it to the patient. That's it."

"Where did the orders come from?"

The pharmacist slowly turned back to his computer screen and clicked a few places. Then, with a quick movement, he grabbed his monitor and turned it towards Edgar. With his left hand, he pointed at the green words.

Order placed by: Harold Palmitieri, MD

Palmitieri thought Edgar. Same last name as Agnus. Daughter of the victim. This was Phyllis' son-in-law. They had met briefly at the crime scene.

"Do you know this 'Harold Palmitieri'?" asked Edgar. He was looking for any breaks in the already failing exterior of this pharmacist.

"I...," began Dr. Andrews. "...do."

There was the in. "How do you know him?"

"Harold and I have worked together since he was a practicing doctor."

"So, he's not a practicing doctor today?"

"No, he's the hospital administrator."

"What did he practice before?"

"Pediatrics."

Edgar wasn't a doctor, but he was pretty certain Parkinson's wasn't a child-based illness, at least in most cases.

"So, answer me this, Dr. Andrews," said Edgar. "Why would a former pediatrician, current hospital administrator send in an order for Ms. Moore—a family member who was not a current patient—for Levodopa? Is that typical?"

"Okay, here's what I know, Detective," Dr. Andrews answered nervously. "All I know is that when Harold came to visit me, he told me that his mother-in-law needed this drug. I didn't ask any questions."

"You are a medical professional. A non-practicing, former pediatrician paid you a visit and told you to administer a highly symptomatic drug to an aging patient, and you simply responded with 'yes'? No questions asked?"

Dr. Andrews nodded his head slowly. Edgar lifted one eyebrow.

"You know that sounds ridiculous, right?"

Dr. Andrews cautiously shrugged his shoulders and offered a half smile as a response. Edgar grabbed his notepad and scribbled ambiguously on a margin. It was a tactic to peak more anxiety from a suspect during interrogation. Oftentimes, worried about their own innocence, they'd start to add more details to try and shift or influence whatever the Detective was writing. It was foolproof.

On cue, Dr. Andrews added, "He told me that they were convinced she had been misdiagnosed. They were getting a second opinion, but in his medical opinion, Levodopa was the best course of action to ease her suffering. I didn't even know she was suffering. I hadn't spoken to her in months. I just did what I was told."

Edgar stopped writing. He slowly lifted his head and squinted his eyes. After a quick scan of the fear-stricken pharmacist, he sighed deeply and put his notepad away. It was enough. He was circling the chum in the water by now.

"Thank you, Dr. That will be all."

Edgar stood up and left the doctor sweating behind the counter with his head in his hand. Before he was able to step away, Dr. Andrews stood up quickly and added, "What does this mean for me? What happened?"

"We'll be in touch," added Edgar before he walked away.

Grabbing the folded stack of papers, he held on to them in his right hand and made his way out the door of the pharmacy and into his vehicle. Sliding into the driver's side, he tossed the paperwork to the passenger seat and watched as the four random sheets of blank paper scattered across the cushion. On top of two of the pages bored the innocuous bold-faced letterhead that read:

Douglas Taylor, Estate Planning

Edgar couldn't help but smile at himself in the mirror as he cranked the ignition.

"Still got it, old man," he whispered as his car turned out into the street.

Chapter 20

"Georgianne, please calm down and talk to me," was all Michael could muster.

The soft hues of tanned skin in his cheeks were drained entirely. All that remained was a ghostlike appearance. Georgianne, on the other hand, was bloodred in her complexion. She had entered her house not 10 minutes before, ready to pounce on whoever dared to cross her.

"I will not calm down, Michael. You haven't answered one single question I've asked since I got here."

"I'm trying to—"

"What is going on between you and my parents?"

Silence. Michael dropped his head. "I can't tell you everything right now. I just can't."

"What do you mean 'you can't tell me'? I'm your fiancé, Michael! And those are my parents."

"I can't, Georgianne!" Michael yelled. "For your own good, I can't! Stop asking me!"

Georgianne's mouth had fallen open. She was stunned. Michael had always been a secure, confident man. It was what drew her to him years before. But now, the man who stood before him in her bedroom was a broken shell of that man. His face was white as a ghost. His cheeks sunken. For the first time, she realized he was skinnier than before.

"Michael," she said softly, grabbing his hand at the wrist. "We are going to be married in less than a year. We can't keep secrets from each other anymore. Especially ones that are eating us alive."

Michael avoided his fiancé's gaze. After a deep sigh, he slowly pushed Georgianne toward the end of the bed, and they both sat. He cleared his throat and then met her eyes. After a quick search, he finally spoke.

"I've done something. Something bad."

Nothing. Georgianne's mouth once again dropped slightly. Her breath quickened.

"When your grandmother passed..."

The door swung open violently. Standing in the doorway, Agnus' eyes bore two deep holes into the shaken Michael's countenance. Allison jumped up reactively as if she had been caught amid some sinister sin.

"Excuse me, mother. Do you knock!"

"What's going on in here?" Agnus asked. Her eyes still trained on Michael.

"I'm talking with my fiancé. You don't have the right to barge in..."

173

"The right?" Agnus coughed hysterically. "Last I checked, and this is my home. You may be an 'adult,' but you live here rent-free. Don't you dare forget that?"

The tension bubbled over in the room. Georgianne caught herself at the last minute before she responded with what was on her mind. She knew that pushing further may result in her ending up homeless.

"Can I speak with you, please? In private?" Agnus asked Michael.

Michael stood up obediently and started moving towards the door. He shot a quick, nervous glance towards his fiancé. Then, Georgianne jumped between the two of them, pushing her hands into both chests as if trying to push down the pillars of Samson's temple.

"Now, just wait a minute. I'm tired of not being included in whatever is going on here."

"We have business with your fiancé, Georgianne. I'm simply trying to conduct it in private as it does not concern you in the slightest."

"' We'?" Allison asked.

"Your father and I," Agnus answered. "Not you."

Michael moved quickly by Georgianne and followed Agnus out to the kitchen. She refused to give up that quickly.

She stayed close behind Michael as the three of them joined Harold in the kitchen.

"I'm not done talking about this, Mother!"

Suddenly, she caught herself before ramming into Michael's back. It was then she noticed everyone was standing still, rigid, around the kitchen island. She wasn't entirely certain, but in the kitchen's warm lighting, it looked like her mother's and father's faces had turned the same white shade that her fiancé's had been all day.

Sitting patiently at the counter was Detective Thomas. In his hand was a notepad, and on his face was a soft grin.

"Detective Thomas?" Georgianne asked. Her parents and Michael were silent.

"Hello, Georgianne," he responded. "How have you been?"

"I'm fine, thank you."

"What's going on?" Agnus piped up.

"Detective Thomas showed up about 15 minutes ago," answered Harold. "He has a few more follow-up questions about your mother's case."

"Oh yeah?" Agnus responded.

"I do," Detective Thomas said. "I hope now is an okay time."

"Well," Agnus began. "Honestly, we were just about to start dinner, so..."

"That's okay," Detective Thomas interrupted. "I won't be long."

Agnus shuffled quickly to her normal place at the sink. There were no dishes to occupy her impatience. For once, Allison thought, maybe her obsession with cleanliness had caught up to her.

"I just had an interesting conversation with Dr. Andrews from the downtown pharmacy. He said you and him were old colleagues?"

Harold nodded. "Yes, I know Andrews. We were in med school together."

"Right, he mentioned that."

Agnus quickly shifted her eyes to Harold, who worked hard to avoid her gaze. Georgianne's mind spun.

What is going on? she thought to herself.

Michael caught himself against the counter as his right leg seemed to shake and give way. He looked sick.

"Are you okay, son?" Detective Thomas asked. "You look like you've witnessed a murder."

"I'm fine," whispered Michael. "I'm just nauseous. I think it was something I ate."

But they hadn't eaten dinner yet. The realization was obvious. The irony was telling.

"Anyway, as I was explaining," continued Detective Thomas. "Dr. Andrews informed me that your husband here, Mrs. Palmitieri, ordered your mother's prescription."

"And?" Agnus answered sharply. "My husband is a doctor."

"Well, actually, he's a hospital administrator. In fact, according to Dr. Andrews, he's an administrator who hasn't practiced medicine in the office in quite some time."

"I still have the ability to write prescriptions, Detective," explained Harold. "I do it often for patients, especially in an emergency."

"I understand that, answered the Detective. "What I don't understand is what 'emergency' happened regarding your mother-in-law for you to prescribe a highly powerful Parkinson's drug. That seems like a very unique medication to prescribe for someone who was clearly not your patient."

Silence. Harold's head lifted slightly as if he was absorbing the revelation.

"What, exactly, are you insinuating, detective?" Agnus piped up.

"I'm simply asking why your husband would need to personally prescribe Levodopa to your mother, Agnus. A drug that obviously caused major hallucinogenic and psychotic episodes in an aging woman who, according to her other medical records, showed no signs of any terminal medical issue. A drug that also was used nearly three times the typical dose in her tea the evening of her death."

"That's it," Agnus yelled. "I've had enough of this. We aren't saying another word until our lawyer is present. You can leave."

The Detective stood up with his shoulders elevated. I understand. You have your rights. I just need you to realize that the walls are closing in on this situation...quickly. If I were you, I would get ahead of it. Save what you can of the consequences."

Michael's head dropped to the counter. It was as if he fainted. Georgianne ran to his back and grabbed him by the shoulders.

"Michael!" she shouted. "Are you okay?"

Michael grunted in response. She felt his forehead. It was clammy and full of cool sweat. Out of habit, the Detective approached the young man and helped Georgianne pull his head off the counter. Michael leaned back into the Detective's chest, and his arms fell forward, palms up. A small black fish tattoo on his right arm peaked out from underneath the sleeve. Detective Thomas' eyes were glued to it.

"That's an interesting tattoo you have there, young man. How long have you had it?"

Shaking off the sickness, Michael looked down and instinctively covered it up.

"I got it a few years back. It was for my—"

"I think you should leave now," Agnus inserted.

The Detective nodded his head as he made his way to the door. "Thank you for your time. I'll be in touch."

With that, he stepped out the door. Georgianne's eyes swelled with tears.

"What is going on!?" she screamed. "Someone better tell me something right now."

Agnus turned abruptly towards her daughter. She came nose to nose with her and stared fiercely.

"Listen to me. Go back to your room and stay quiet."

"I will not! You can't—"

"Leave! Now!" Agnus screamed.

Georgianne couldn't help but look shocked. It was unlike her mother. She may have been a difficult, serious person, but she never yelled. She was too refined for that. Now, for the first time in her memory, her mother had nearly shattered her eardrums with a shaken voice that appeared on the verge of breaking. It was enough to force her to comply. After a quick scan, she turned around and retreated to her bedroom, slamming the door behind her for effect.

Trembling, she grabbed her phone and dialed her cousin's number.

"Allison?" she whispered.

"Georgianne? What's wrong?"

"I..." she began. The words were simply not there. "I...I don't know."

"Do you need me to come over?"

"No. Don't come over."

"Georgianne, you're scaring me. What's going on?"

Silence. Georgianne knew that calling her cousin this way was a mistake. She didn't really know what was going on. Anything she tried to explain right now would only make Allison confused and angry. But she had no one else. Her own fiancé was hiding something. She just knew it. So many times, she had confided in him. Had shared her heart with him. Had been vulnerable with him about her faith and her newfound call to ministry. Things she was afraid to mention to her parents. And now?

There was a light knock on her bedroom door.

"Georgianne?" sounded Michael through the door. His voice sounded muted, hollow even.

"Allison, let me call you back."

She clicked the phone off and hid underneath the pillow that sat next to her. She wasn't sure why she did that. She had nothing to hide.

"Georgianne, can I come in?"

"Not unless you plan on telling me something I don't know!"

She screamed it so the whole house could hear her.

"I plan to."

Georgianne stood up quickly. She had little faith in what her fiancé said, but this was something she hadn't imagined hearing. Was the truth finally coming out? Would she finally be able to get to the bottom of all this?

She opened the door and walked quickly back to her bed, building distance between herself and the broken shell of the man she loved. Michael slowly entered the room, head bowed slightly. He turned his back to Georgianne and quietly closed the door shut. After a second, he finally turned around and leaned against the door.

Georgianne was impatient. "Well? Let's hear it. What's going on, Michael?"

Michael sighed deeply and made his way to the bed. With some noticeable distance between himself and his enraged fiancé, he carefully sat down and laid his hands, palm down, on his legs.

"Georgianne, I'm so sorry about all this."

"Honestly, Michael. I don't care about your apologies right now. I just want to know what is going on in my own home. What happened out there is not right."

"I know. I know," he repeated as if making sure his words were carefully selected. "Your parents did something, Georgianne. And I helped them do it."

"What?" Georgianne's voice broke. Whatever it was had made her once carefree, strong-willed husband-to-be a shadow of the man he was. She wasn't sure she was ready for the truth.

"While your grandmother was alive, your mom facilitated the sale of her house."

"Right."

"The total was...substantial. As far as your family knew, the amount of the home sale would be willed evenly between your aunt, uncles, and your mom. But that wasn't what happened."

"What do you mean?"

"Before your grandmother died, your mom used her Power of Attorney to transfer the full value of the home sale into her account upon her death. This was allowed because the language of the home sale never made it into the will."

"So, mom manipulated her mother months before she died."

"Yes," replied Michael.

"Well, that's not entirely shocking. But what does that have to do with you?"

"I was responsible for adding your mother's name as beneficiary to the mortgage proceeds. Because I had access to the account, I did it without asking questions."

Silence. Georgianne stood up and brushed off her pants leg as if shaking something unwanted from her trousers. The room was spinning slowly. The information was so much, so odd. So, unlike the person she thought she was marrying.

"I don't understand, Michael. What was in this for you? Why would you allow my mother to do this."

"My hands were tied, Georgianne. Your mother had Power of Attorney. She was in control of all decision-making regarding your grandmother's assets while she was alive. As a banker, I had no choice."

"But you could have reported it. You could have told someone! You didn't. You just sat there and let her steal all that money from her siblings. From her mother. And what? For nothing!"

Michael stared quickly at the floor. Georgianne noticed.

"For nothing, right!? Michael! For nothing, right!?"

Michael softly shook his head. Georgianne seethed.

"Of course. You got a cut. How much? 100 k? 200? Was it worth it!?"

"I did it for us, Georgianne. To help with the wedding. To give you a life!"

"I have a life, Michael. A future. One built on truth and morals. Not one rooted in lies and deceit."

She stormed to her door and opened it. Before leaving, she turned back and glared at him.

"I'm not mad at Mom and Dad, Michael. I expect this type of terrible behavior from them. What I never expected was the man I love to help them. Keep your money. I don't want a dime."

Michael waited quietly in Georgianne's bedroom. Faintly, he heard her scream something inaudible at her parents before slamming the front door behind her. The silence that followed was almost peaceful. A grain of solitude and contemplation during weeks of internal torment.

Then, like a church bell in a small town, the peace was split in half as Agnus appeared in her daughter's doorway, arms crossed.

"Well?"

"I did it. She bought it. It's over."

"Yeah, I noticed."

With that, she disappeared. Michael lay backward and fell on the bed beneath him. The chaos reappeared, filling his broken mind and soul with worry and fear. The story was not yet over. He was far from out of the woods.

Nothing had changed. Well, except now, he had one angry fiancé.

Chapter 21

Arlene paused before ringing the doorbell to her right. It had taken everything in her not to bang on the door with a closed fist. For the first time since she received her ALS diagnosis, she could sense a boiling anger rising in her chest. She had promised herself then that she would never react in such a way again. She had too much faith in her Heavenly Father to allow circumstances in her life to control her emotions like that.

Today, however, that same old feeling came back with a vengeance. She breathed deeply. Silently, she prayed to God for guidance. Wisdom.

Like a wisp of cool air, she heard a whisper in the breeze say, "Vengeance is mine."

"Yes, Lord," she whispered back. Her heart rate settled. She softly pushed the doorbell and waited.

What felt like two whole minutes passed, and finally, the door opened before she stood her sister, as prim and proper as she always was. Not a hair amiss or a wrinkle on her blouse.

"Hello, Agnus."

"Arlene, I can't talk. I was just heading—"

Arlene pushed past her with her cane and walked in anyway. Agnus was visibly taken aback by the intrusion.

"Excuse me, you can't just walk in—"

"Sit down, Agnus. We need to talk."

It was confidence that Agnus had never heard from her sister before. Not even when they were younger. For the first time in a long time, she complied with her older sister's command.

Sitting across the kitchen bar from her sister, Arlene leaned forward and stared intently into Agnus' eyes.

"What is going on?" Agnus asked indignantly.

"You tell me, Agnus."

"Tell you what?"

"Agnus, it's time we stopped playing games. I know about the house sale and how you swindled the trust out of all the proceeds. How did you use Georgianne's fiancé to set up the bank accounts? What I don't understand is 'why.' Why would you do that? Do that to your own family?"

"Let me guess. You heard all of this from my emotional daughter, who just left my house after getting into a big fight with her fiancé. Is that correct?"

"Agnus," Arlene answered. "It's time you stop playing games and be honest. For once in your life, be honest."

"For once in my life!?" screamed Agnus. "For once in my life!? I have been nothing but honest to this entire God-forsaken family since we lost Dad. The day you were no longer held accountable for anything due to your diagnosis, I had to step up and run this family. So, yeah. The house proceeds went to me. Every dime. Not because I wanted to cheat the family. But because I earned every bit of it! Our brothers have been AWOL since Dad died, and you have been useless!"

The words stung like bullets. Arlene felt her lip quiver automatically under the weight of the accusations. Then that same steadied resolve that strengthened her outside the door earlier returned. She breathed in deeply and settled her nerves before responding.

"I know you have done a lot, Agnus. No one would argue that. But you know as well as I do that that money was meant for all of us."

"Just like the extra money you received, Arlene?"

Arlene's eyes bulged.

"Yeah, don't think I don't know it," continued Agnus. "I did the math. There's no way you had enough from your inheritance to pay for Allison's schooling and your once-in-a-lifetime surgery. So, tell me, how did you get the money?"

Arlene gritted her teeth. She knew it would come out some way or another, but she wasn't prepared for the attack.

"Agnus, our parents put money aside for my care. I didn't ask for it, nor did I steal it from the trust."

"' Your care,'" repeated Agnus with a sinister voice. "That's all I've ever heard about. 'Your care!' I'm so tired of poor little Arlene and her 'care.' Admit it, Arlene! You stole from the trust! You murdered our mother for the money!"

Arlene's mouth dropped. How on Earth could anyone suspect this? Not only was it physically impossible, but it would be unthinkable. What was her sister doing?

"Agnus, what is happening to you? What is all this? You know for a fact that I would never hurt our mother. What are you trying to pull?"

Agnus crossed her arms and stared fiercely at her sister. The expression was forced, rehearsed almost. She wasn't fooling anyone. Arlene leaned forward. Within her spirit, she felt the presence of the Lord rises in her. It pushed her forward, calmed her senses, and even steadied her reflexes.

Softly, she asked, "Agnus, did you do something to mom?"

Agnus stood up abruptly and turned towards the sink. There were no dishes. No distractions. She sighed and turned back to Arlene.

"I think you should leave."

"Agnus, answer the question. Did you hurt mom?"

"Arlene! I'm only going to say this one more time: You need to leave my home now!"

Arlene sat back and soaked in the situation. It felt like boiling water. Did her sister really kill their mother? Was she covering this up? So many questions. So much anxiety. Her head was spinning. To avoid further issues, she pushed the chair back and reached for her cane. Slowly, she brought herself up to stand and looked at her sister.

"Agnus, you may not believe in God like I do. Or like mom did. But you know His power. You know His truth. It's how you were raised."

Agnus said nothing. Arlene grabbed her pocketbook and placed it on her shoulder.

"' Be sure your sins will find you out,'" quoted Arlene as she turned and made her way to the door.

Before she stepped out the door, she turned back to Agnus, who hadn't moved.

"What's hidden in the darkness will come to light. Guaranteed."

Arlene made her way to the taxi and entered the vehicle. Her hands were shaking, and her heart was pounding. She wasn't sure what to do with what she knew. There was nothing admitted. Nothing certain. But in her heart, she knew the truth.

Her sister had something to do with her mother's death. And she needed to do something about it.

"Detective Thomas, please," Arlene's voice sounded over the office phone. The receptionist answered with a polite, "Hold please" and transferred the call. Edgar was busy pouring his third cup of black coffee in the breakroom when the receptionist called.

"Arlene on line 3," her voice rang down the hall.

This investigation had dragged out long enough that now the receptionist and key witnesses were on a first name basis. The thought made Edgar shake his head softly.

We're getting close, he reassured himself.

He shuffled towards his office door and shut it behind him. Picking up the receiver, he grabbed his notebook and prepared himself before clicking the line.

"Ms. Arlene," he answered. "How are you?"

"It was her, Detective Thomas."

"It was who?"

"Agnus." Arlene paused. Edgar could tell this was difficult. "My sister did something to my mother."

"I understand," Edgar responded, trying to sound calm and kind. "Why do you feel that way?"

Arlene began unraveling her tale about Agnus and Harold and the money that they pocketed from the sale of the house. She explained that with a power of attorney at her disposal, Agnus controlled the assets of her mother's estate and manipulated her every move. She then proceeded to rouse suspicion regarding Agnus' control over Phyllis' medication and Harold's access to prescriptions.

None of it was new. This is what frustrated Edgar more than anything. When Arlene finally paused to catch her breath, Edgar stepped back in.

"Arlene, I know you are hurting right now. And I'm not saying that what you are telling me isn't true. It may very well be. But unfortunately, we can't pin the death of your mother on Agnus because she pocketed the house sale. We looked at their bank records. It's wrong, but it's legal. We also have found nothing that would suggest now that your sister was the one who fed your mother an overdose of Levodopa. The timeline checks out."

"But the cup! She tried to clean the cup until your detective stopped--!"

"What this does do, Arlene," Edgar continued. "Is further remove you from any suspicion."

Edgar could cut the tension over the phone with a knife. He could tell that the last statement shocked Arlene. It almost made him feel guilty even saying it. Unfortunately, the millions she received right around the same time her mother was found dead drew a scary, bold line from Phyllis' death and Arlene's motive. However, her story, paperwork, and continued communication worked in her favor. This conversation was no different.

"At first, the additional funds you received around the time of your mother's death were suspicious. My team checked out the paperwork your lawyer provided—Taylor—and it was all legit. The date stamps were before Phyllis' death, and so was his story corroborating your receipt of the funds before then. Your alibi is clear."

"Well, I'm glad to hear I didn't murder my mother!" Arlene yelled, crying on the phone.

Up to this point, she had been a portrait of grace and patience. The break in her voice alarmed Edgar more than any case had done in quite some time. His heart broke.

"Did you talk to Douglas? He and my mother had a conversation right before she passed. He was worried about her. I'm sure that would help."

"We talked briefly, and he shared some of his concerns regarding your sister. We didn't have any conversation. I honestly don't know if he trusted me too much at that point."

"I can talk with him. Let him know you are genuine. He's a good man! He always loved my parents."

"I could see that," agreed Edgar. "I don't mind talking with him again. I do want to talk to you about something else. Some new evidence has been brought forward. When we noticed the hallway cameras were off the night before her death, we subpoenaed the residence to provide camera footage from the month leading up to the incident. It took a long time for them to respond, but our lab just received it yesterday. My team has been scouring the footage all night."

"Did you find anything?"

"Well, we found one thing. Right before they turned off, there was a figure who messed with the lenses. We never caught a face or even a body, just a hand and wrist."

"That doesn't sound like a lot."

"Well, it's not. Except for one small detail that my guys noticed late last night. A fish tattoo on the figure's right wrist."

Nothing. Edgar realized this detail wasn't very important to Arlene. Maybe she had never gotten close to her niece's fiancé before.

"What's interesting about this is that there was another instance on one of the doorbell cameras earlier in the case where a black-dressed figure walked in front with the same tattoo on the same wrist."

"What does this mean, detective?"

"Arlene, your niece, Georgianne's fiancé, Michael. Have you ever met him?"

"A couple of times."

"Well, when I paid a visit to your sister's home a few nights ago, I noticed a small fish tattoo, just like the one in the video, on his wrist. His right wrist."

"Michael? Do you think he has something to do with my mother's death?"

"I can't say for sure yet. But I wanted to ask you if you have ever noticed anything about Michael and your sister. Any strange behavior? Maybe conspiracy or planning?"

"Never. Like I've said, I've only seen him a couple of times. If you feel this man has done something, why not arrest him? Why not bring him in for questioning?"

"We are working on it, Arlene. I promise."

"You need to work harder, Detective! Please! I can't handle this!"

"Arlene, please. Take a breath—"

"Take a breath!? I've been breathing since my mother was murdered, Detective! I haven't stopped. She, however, can no longer draw breath. And now, you feel like you may have a murderer and are telling me to take another breath!"

"I'm so sorry, Arlene. I know you are hurting."

"Detective Thomas, I don't mean to be angry. I'm not angry at you. I'm just upset. I know you are trying."

"You don't owe me an apology."

"I have a request, Detective. If I may,"

"What's that?"

"Can I sit in on the next interrogation? It doesn't sound like I'm a suspect anymore, but I want to see how Michael and Agnus respond to this. I don't know if that's allowed, but if it's possible..."

It wasn't necessarily wrong. It just wasn't normal. But, in the past few weeks, nothing was normal about this case.

"I will see what I can do," answered Edgar. "It's not a normal thing we do, but I can see."

Another pause. Edgar swallowed his next sentence. He could tell Arlene was frantic. Upset. And frankly, he wasn't too far from it either. After he gathered his thoughts, he whispered a small prayer. Something he hadn't done in a long time. Like cool water, peace overwhelmed him, and he remembered how important faith was to Arlene. This was a woman whom he secretly admired. A woman of courage and fortitude. He sighed quickly and lowered his tone.

"Arlene, listen to me. I never make promises I can't fully commit to keeping. It's a part of this job. Sometimes, evil wins. There's nothing we can do about it. But—" he let the pause linger on the phone. "I promise you this. We will get to the bottom of your mother's death. Once and for all. You have my word."

Arlene sat with the promise for what felt like an eternity on the other end of the phone. Edgar counted his breaths and swirled his black coffee cup in his right hand while he waited out of respect. Finally, she sighed heavily and responded.

"Detective Thomas. Thank you for everything. I believe you will try your hardest. I really do. But at this point, with all due respect, my faith is in my Heavenly Father. He will be vindicated."

Edgar nodded on his side of the conversation. No one saw it, of course, but he felt obligated to make his next sentence count.

"Then, Ms. Arlene, let's let Him work."

Chapter 22

Edgar Thomas gripped the steering wheel tightly. His heart was pounding. Carefully, he walked through the evidence in his mind.

1. The tox report. A dosage three times the normal volume of Levodopa was found in the cup that Agnus had attempted to clean at the crime scene.
2. Harold Palmitieri was the doctor who ordered the drug four months earlier for Phyllis Moore.
3. A darkly clothed individual in the shape of a tall man sporting a fish tattoo passed by the adjoining doorbell camera next to Phyllis' apartment the night of her death.

He sipped his coffee slowly. Quietly, he played the conversation he had just had with Douglas Taylor through his mind.

Edgar: Arlene mentioned you had spoken with Phyllis just before she died. Can you elaborate on what you talked about?

Douglas: It was about three weeks before it all happened. She called me nervous about her mental state. She was worried that things were getting worse and that she

would make a financial mistake before it was too late.

Edgar: What was she concerned with exactly?

Douglas: She said it was her medication. Agnus and

Harold had been giving her a dose of medication each night

before bed. She said it would cause her to act loopy and tired.

She would almost faint every time. I remember her saying that

when she took it, her day was done. She was useless after the

fact until the next morning.

Edgar: And the figures she kept seeing?

Douglas: She was convinced someone was stalking her.

But she was too nervous to say anything because of the

medication. Agnus had convinced her she was going crazy, and

no one would believe her.

In just a few moments, Michael, the boyfriend of

Georgianne Palmitieri, the daughter of Harold and Agnus,

would arrive for questioning. His lawyer, a local criminal

defense attorney named George Carmichael, would be in tow.

This is the moment, thought Edgar. It all comes down

to this.

He shook off the conversation with the lawyer and

thought through the next steps. His plan was simple. Share the

facts as they are presented, withholding key details until the most opportune time. Considering the state that Michael was in at the Palmitieri home a few days prior, his hope was he wouldn't need much coaxing to confess. What precisely he would confess to was still up in the air. But Edgar was optimistic.

Edgar put his coffee down in the cup holder and reached his right hand into his bag. Blindly, he retrieved the folded piece of thin paper. The subpoena. This time, a real one. Edgar smiled at the memory from the pharmacy.

After another quick breath in, he finally turned the car off and headed towards the station entrance. When he walked in, Michael was already waiting for him.

"Hello, there!" exclaimed Edgar. "You're early!"

Michael stood and shook Edgar's hand. "Yeah, I couldn't wait any longer."

"Your lawyer on their way?"

Michael shook his head. "No lawyer. I just want to get this over with."

Edgar escorted Michael through the door and pointed to his office down the hall. When Michael stepped forward, Edgar doubled back and whispered to the receptionist.

"Did the—"

The receptionist nodded and quietly responded, "Arlene and her daughter and niece came by right before Michael showed up. We already sent them to the viewing room. No one saw anything."

Edgar sighed deeply and nodded back. It was a good thing. Had Georgianne met Michael Thin in the lobby before this interrogation, the whole thing would have been blown. Now, they can watch quietly, and Michael will be none the wiser.

In the small cinder block room, the two men grabbed a seat.

"Do you want anything? Water? Coffee?"

"No, thank you," Michael whispered.

"Okay, so the reason I have you here is to ask you a—"

"Let me stop you there." Michael's face was white again. But Edgar noticed he had more strength in his neck and shoulders than he had back at Agnus' house. "This won't take long."

"Oh?" Edgar leaned back in his chair. In his hand, he held his notebook and pen.

"At Georgianne's, you asked me about my tattoo. Why?"

"I noticed it on your hand. It seemed odd on a businessman such as yourself."

"I got it when I was a teenager. After my father died."

Edgar nodded his head.

"It stands for faith. For Jesus. Mom and Dad always had me in church growing up. It wasn't until I became an adult that I decided to quit going. Wasn't for me."

Michael stared at the little tattoo and rubbed it absentmindedly.

"Well, we all change as we get older. It's understandable..."

"Sorry," Michael interrupted. "I don't mean to cut you off, but I didn't just 'change.' I gave up."

"Sorry? Gave up what?"

"I gave up on everything I once believed. Faith, truth. Integrity. At first, I thought it was the financial industry. Maybe college. My MBA. But it was earlier than that. I just...I just quit believing."

Edgar remained silent. He wasn't sure where Michael was heading, but he felt like a breakthrough was lurking around the corner. Maybe I won't have to question after all.

"Detective," Michael continued. "Georgianne's grandmother wasn't as sick as her mother wanted her to believe. I'm not sure she was sick at all."

"What do you mean?"

Another pause. The next words looked like they hurt Michael.

"About six months before Ms. Phyllis died, Agnus approached me about a business opportunity. She told me that the money to be made could more than pay for my and Georgianne's wedding and would set us up for a few strong years in our bank account. She called it her and Harold's 'wedding gift' for us. Of course, I was excited about the idea of making money. I always looked for ways to make more money.

The plan was...involved. Agnus had already taken over Phyllis' accounts and gotten the POA approved by the courts. She was making moves financially to shore up all the family assets in the case of Phyllis' passing. She also had taken over Phyllis' medical care. That's where Harold came in. They had found out about the drug Levodopa after Phyllis had a doctor's appointment for her restless legs. I guess the drug can be used for that, but only in short stints. Harold took over the prescription, and they decided to get the hospital to put the word 'Parkinson's' in her file."

"This is how she was able to take it for as long as she did?" asked Edgar.

"Yes," nodded Michael. "It was Harold's way of justifying the refills."

"So, what happened next?"

"Then it was my turn. Because Levodopa can cause hallucinations in older patients, Agnus hatched this elaborate plan to push Phyllis to her breaking point. My job was to show up, dressed in black, and scare her. A couple of times, I would go to her house and stand in the backyard. Agnus gave me a key to the gate. Phyllis would get scared and call her family, and I would disappear without a trace."

"That explains the intruder at her house," Edgar added.

"Right. The plan was to have her go crazy and deem her mentally unfit to make any decisions. But it didn't work right away. And Agnus got impatient. That's when the house was sold, and Phyllis was moved to the retirement home."

"Did Phyllis kill herself, Michael?"

Silence. Now, Edgar noticed the same slumping of the neck and shoulders. Whatever was about to come out was killing this young man.

"No," was all Michael said.

Edgar let the 'no' linger in the room for a moment. When nothing else came after it, he prodded further.

"Michael, what happened the night that Phyllis fell to her death?"

Tears streamed from Michael's eyes. His shoulders trembled under the weight of his confession.

"I did what I was told to do. I only meant to scare her. I waited in the hallway until Agnus left and opened the door. I slipped in after she left and hid in Phyllis' kitchen while she went back to her room. When she came back out, she saw me standing in the kitchen."

Michael started heaving, crying hysterically.

"Michael, what happened when she came out and saw you?" asked Edgar softly.

"She freaked out. I didn't know what to do. I expected her to get scared, but she ran straight for the sliding glass door. She threw it open and leaned against the railing, trying to get away. But there was nowhere to go. I saw her start to fall backward and run after her. This scared her even more, and she fell."

There was a small hum from the vending machine right down the hall from Edgar's office. The noise leaked from underneath the closed door. It was the only thing I heard.

"Okay, so let me get this straight. When you approached Phyllis, she—"

"I killed her, Detective. I killed Phyllis Moore."

Arlene gripped her daughter's shoulder tightly. She watched painfully as Georgianne sat on the edge of the table, mouth suspended in a look of awe and pain. The revelation washed over the three women as the speaker clicked off. Through the one-sided window, they watched as Michael stood up and an officer placed the metal cuffs on each wrist. His face was distraught, distorted. It was as if he saw a ghost.

Then Arlene realized he was looking at the window. Of course, he couldn't see them, only his reflection as he was cuffed and processed.

He is seeing a ghost, she thought.

Georgianne's shoulders heaved heavily. Allison ran to her side and covered her in an embrace. Arlene could see the reality setting in like a poison ingested. Slowly. Insidiously. All the dirty, terrible details about her family were being revealed, and she had a front-row seat. Arlene shifted towards her niece's side and patted her back slowly. Words weren't enough.

It was a good thing, too. Arlene was out of things to say.

Booking Michael was painless. There was no fight. He complied with all orders. His confession was transcribed, and he signed the bottom of the page clearly and elegantly. Edgar couldn't help but see the irony. He had never met a banker with good handwriting.

Michael, on the other hand, was no ordinary banker. He was a murderer.

Edgar sat back in his chair and contemplated what had happened. The feeling of "cracking the case" eluded him. This almost felt too easy. Michael, after all, was a good kid. He was just a victim of greed and poor judgment. To Edgar, it didn't feel like he was locking away a terrible person or a threat to society. There was no satisfaction in what had happened in that interrogation room. Only an empty book ends in a large, unending case.

But a murderer was now behind bars. It was a good thing. But empty. Edgar was convinced the real threat was still abroad. Unfortunately, Michael's confession only indicted one person.

There was still work to be done to put Agnus Palmitieri behind bars.

Chapter 23

News spread quickly of Michael's arrest. That night, Georgianne came home, packed her bags, and screamed violently at Harold and his wife for what felt like hours. Harold had never been a very affectionate father, but he loved his daughter. To see her like this, accusing him and Agnus of conspiring with Michael and murdering his mother-in-law, was a difficult thing to endure. Partly because of the betrayal in Georgianne's eyes and partly because of the heavy truth that stood behind it all.

When Georgianne slammed the door behind her, he and Agnus had decided it would be wise to call into work the next day. He sent his assistant a text and shot a few emails from his personal computer. To everyone at the hospital, Harold was "sick."

That evening, the wine stayed in the cupboard and the glasses on the shelf while Agnus and Harold plotted their next move. They knew they couldn't stick around too closely for too long. The proceeds from the house sale had already tripled in value since the investment was made, and their account was large. It was a perfect time to book a flight and head to Moscow. Harold had built a contact there, and, of course, there was no extradition treaty. The plan felt foolproof, but still, Harold couldn't shake the panic that was forming in his chest. Nothing seemed to help.

What made it worse, too, was the guilt. Harold was not a bad person at heart. Of course, he had always valued the dollar over most things. But he remembered a time when money had less of a draw on him. It was during medical school when he was a resident. He loved the feeling of assisting young people and parents. He enjoyed the satisfaction that came from giving answers to frazzled mothers and fathers over their ailing newborns.

Truth be told, he hadn't felt that satisfaction for a long time. And now, as he watched his wife furiously shove clothes into a suitcase, all he felt was a toxic mixture of regret, shame, and disgust.

"What do we do with the mutual funds?" Agnus asked.

"What do you mean?"

"Well, I'm sure it's only a matter of time before the cops seize our accounts. Especially if Michael said anything about our involvement, I plan to take as much as I can out of our checking at the bank tomorrow. The rest is in our offshore accounts. But last I saw, we still had a quarter million in our mutual funds. What do we need to do with that?"

"I can call Brad at the firm and have him liquidate it into our offshore accounts. It'll take some time, but it should work. The biggest amount, though, is in our checking."

This satisfied Agnus enough to keep packing. Harold sat on the side of the bed and stared blankly. His thoughts began to wander again. This time, he thought of the paper trail with his name on it at the hospital. The pharmacy's records showed him clearly prescribing the Levodopa to Phyllis. Though his story was effective enough in throwing the Detective off the scent, now he wasn't so sure anymore. It was a smoking gun. He had no business prescribing anything that powerful to his aging mother-in-law.

"Agnus, we need to talk through this."

"There's nothing to talk about, Harold," snapped Agnus as she zipped up her suitcase. "We stick to the plan. That's what we do. I'll get the cash-out tomorrow, and you can put in your resignation. Period. The flight takes off at 5."

Resignation. The word stung. Eight years of college and five grueling years of residency. Not to mention the decades spent climbing the ladder at the hospital to reach his current level. It was a lot of time. It was a lot of energy.

And now, it was all going away so he could hide in a foreign country with his fugitive wife and the money he made from conspiring against his mother-in-law.

Agnus could tell he was struggling internally. Not normally one for affection or compassion, Harold watched as she awkwardly tried to console him. Of course, the goal was to make him comply, not to make him feel good about it. This wasn't lost on him at all.

"Harold, listen," she said with a short, quick tone, albeit with a hint of softness. "In a few days, we will be free of this. We'll have a new life with plenty of money. All of this will be behind us. You just have to hold it together for a short while longer. Can you do that?"

Harold winced against the patronizing question. "Yes, Agnus. I can do that. I've been doing that this whole time. I did that when you forgot the cup at your mother's. I did that when you acted suspiciously in front of the Detective. I'll keep doing that until this is put to rest."

"Good," snapped Agnus. "Now finish packing and get some rest."

With that, she disappeared into the kitchen, shutting off the bedroom light as she exited. Harold was left alone, sitting in the darkness. He didn't move. The room instantly filled with a heavy oppression. To this point, he had kept the remorse and regret at bay. He acted like a surgeon, calm and steady. But now, as the shadows extended from the closed bedroom window, filling the room with a smothering void of heavy darkness, the gates burst. He felt the first tear in years trace his chin.

What have we done? he thought to himself. And for what? Money?

Finally, a question without an answer. A thought without a plan. Harold was vulnerable and frightened. A feeling he was certain Phyllis had felt that night on the balcony.

The next day was a dark one. Clouds hung overhead as Agnus entered the bank building. She knew she was panicking. But she couldn't help it. Michael had failed her, Harold was too scared to leave the house, and she was sure her name was brought up in the confession. The only thing she had control over was the money.

Just a week earlier, the profit from the investment was liquidated. In her account stood a cool $900 thousand. It was exposed, available, and ripe for the taking. Agnus was still finalizing her plan when the person before her was called to the teller.

Withdraw $250k this morning. Get to Russia tomorrow and take the remainder out there. By this time tomorrow, the rest will be history and they will have a Russian account with no access to the States.

"I can help the next guest!" the teller yelled from behind the counter.

Agnus compartmentalized the information and resumed her air of confidence. Her head tilted back and her chin forward. Now was not the time to act guilty. She was still in charge.

"I need to make a substantial withdrawal from my savings."

"Yes, ma'am," the teller responded. "How much will you be taking?"

"$250,000."

The teller's eyes bulged. Agnus had to stifle her irritation.

"That's quite a bit! Are you sure you wouldn't want to—"

"I want my money now," Agnus answered flatly. She steadied herself quietly. The last thing she needed to do was draw attention.

"Understood. Let me get my manager to assist."

The teller disappeared behind the counter. Moments later, the bank manager appeared with a curious gaze.

"Hello, Mrs. Palmitieri. How are you doing today?"

"Jonathon, I'm not here to have a conversation. I want my money. Now."

"I understand, Mrs. Palmitieri. Unfortunately, a sum like that requires additional screening on my end. I'll need to ask you a few questions and have you sign some paperwork before we can proceed."

"That's not necessary. I just want my money."

"I'm sorry, ma'am. But this is a federal requirement. It won't take too long."

Agnus felt sweat form on her brow and upper lip. Her heart screamed in her chest. Out of the corner of her eye, she saw the police officer shift in his chair. More than likely, it was just to get comfortable, but to Agnus—right now—everything was about her.

"So, Mrs. Palmitieri, can we ask what the purpose of this withdrawal is?"

"None of your business," she snarled.

"Mrs. Palmitieri, you don't have to be specific. Just in general. Is it for personal? Business? Real Estate?"

"Personal."

She saw the manager's face twist. It dawned on her: $250,000 for personal is a red flag.

Stupid answer, Agnus.

The next few questions were more formal and easier to answer. Agnus tried her best to appear natural. She felt like she was succeeding. Until...

"Mrs. Palmitieri, are you feeling okay?"

She realized she was sweating profusely. When asked the question, she shifted unsteadily on her feet. She felt the color drain from her face.

"I'm—I'm fine."

The teller shot a quick glance at the officer, who noticed the exchange himself. He had already made it halfway over when Agnus steadied herself against the counter.

"I've had enough of this! It's my money! Give me my money!"

"Excuse me, ma'am. You need to calm down," the officer interjected.

"I'm not going to calm down! This bank is refusing to give me my money! I've worked hard for that money. If I wanted a million dollars, I have the right to receive it! Now, back off and let me get my money!"

The officer reached up to his radio and whispered a cryptic phrase. Through the haze of her panic and distress, Agnus thought she heard the words "back up" come out of his mouth.

"Oh really!? You think I'm dangerous!"

Before she realized it, she reached out and struck the officer in the chest. Within seconds, she was pressed against the teller window with her hands behind her back.

"You're under arrest...right to remain silent...court will appoint..." The officer's words faded in and out. Agnus felt her grasp over this situation falling slowly to the ground. Up to this point, she had avoided detainment and threatened with her lawyer. Now, she was under arrest for disturbing the peace and obstruction of justice.

Chapter 24

It was the same tiny room it had been just a day before. The feeling of déjà vu was hard to shake. Arlene settled into the uncomfortable metal chair and beside her, her daughter and her niece. In front of them, a cold one-way mirror that revealed a small table with Agnus chained to a metal loop.

Georgianne was hysterical, trying her best to stifle her sobs on Allison's shoulder. In just two short days, her fiancé had been arrested for breaking and entering and second-degree murder, and now her mother was detained for being a public nuisance at a bank. When the Detective had called Arlene just hours earlier, he also described how there was a high chance that Harold would be detained for suspicion of fleeing. Like dominos, this young woman's entire world was falling around her. Arlene's heart was crushed when she broke the news to her niece.

But still, Georgianne demanded that she attend the interrogation. It was a miracle they were there, to begin with, and none of the women wanted to waste it. Arlene watched as Agnus sighed defiantly in the chair. She crossed her legs like a high-class lady and looked around the room with an air of arrogance. If she wasn't mistaken, it almost looked to Arlene like her sister was bored of it all. This made her blood boil. Truth be told, Arlene was thankful a concrete wall and ballistic glass were standing between her and Agnus. Despite her slowly dilapidating body and diminishing motor skills, she felt enough vitriol that she was certain she could do some damage to her sister before the cops intervened.

Vengeance is mine, she heard a voice whisper. It sounded like her mother's. But Arlene knew it wasn't. It was a reminder from the Holy Spirit. A recall of the scripture found in Deuteronomy:

Vengeance is mine, I will repay, saith the Lord.

It was the same scripture her pastor had read in his sermon on forgiveness the Sunday before. She remembered resting on that truth while she listened to the message over live stream. It was a calming reassurance. A reminder of God's perfect timing.

"God had this under control," she whispered to the room. "He'll never forsake us, girls. Trust in that."

Allison looked at her mother and nodded her head. Georgianne wiped her tears and laid her head on Arlene's shoulder.

"I believe it, Aunt Arlene," she whispered back. "I believe it."

"Don't say a word unless I tell you to. I'll do the talking."

George Carmichael was a sleazy individual with a slicked back, jet-black hair, and a pencil mustache that crawled along his upper lip. His suit was tailored carefully, and his shoes shined so brightly the halogen lights almost flickered when he shifted his feet.

"So far, the only thing they have on you is a disorderly conduct charge. We can reduce it to a misdemeanor, and you'll be out of here in a couple of hours. The cops are on their way to get Harold. We will need him to do the same to avoid anything."

Just then, Detective Thomas appeared in the interrogation room. Grabbing his seat carefully, he leaned forward and crossed his arms.

"Hello, Agnus. How are you feeling?"

"My client refuses to answer any questions irrelevant to the matter at hand," explained George.

"Understood. It says here that you were detained after becoming hostile when the bank asked questions regarding your withdrawal. Is that correct?"

"My client voiced her opinion, and the officer in the bank took it as hostile. There is no proof that what she did or didn't do was deemed hostile."

"It says here in the arrest report that she was yelling loudly and refusing to comply when asked to calm down and that she struck the officer. Is that correct, Agnus?"

"Don't answer that," George interrupted.

"That's fine," continued the Detective. "I do have a question to ask. The teller explained that you were looking to withdraw $250,000 in cash. Is that correct?"

"That has nothing to do with why she is being detained," explained George.

"Well," Detective Thomas answered. "That's not entirely true. On the arrest report, it appears that a report was filed to the IRS in accordance with the Bank Secrecy Act for the amount attempting to be withdrawn. This falls under the USA Patriot Act. I'm well within my rights as an officer of the law to ask your client what the nature of this transaction was for."

George wrinkled his forehead. He was caught. He turned to face Agnus and nodded.

"You can answer, but don't feel obligated to give this man any details. He can take you to court if he really wants an answer."

"I wanted the money that I earned. Period," Agnus responded.

"You earned?"

"Right! Earned! It's my money!"

"That's interesting. Because after you were arrested, we pulled your bank statements, and it looks like this money was distributed from a holding account that came from your son-in-law, Michael."

Agnus's eyes bulged. That wasn't supposed to be traceable.

"We had a joint investment together. Michael assisted with transactions, and we split the profit. It was all legal."

"Legal? You mean, your banker son-in-law who just confessed to receiving money from you and your husband as a result of scaring your aging mother to her death?"

"Okay, we've had enough of this. Agnus, get your things," George insisted.

"My mother was sick!" Agnus screamed. Her inhibitions were shaking loose.

"Agnus, stop," George interjected.

"No, you stop! I'm tired of all this! I'm innocent!"

"Agnus, your mother was not sick!" interjected the Detective. "She was old. The medicine you kept feeding her made her sick."

"My mother was sick long before she received that medicine. She was sick in the head! All she cared about was her church. She was sitting on a goldmine left behind by my father, and she didn't spend a dime of it. Then, Arlene got sick, and I was left to handle her affairs. Her accounts were in shambles when I took over! She gave thousands to that church and thousands more to Arlene's medical bills! If I hadn't stopped her, she would have spent every dime of my inheritance!"

Detective Thomas's eyes widened. "' Stopped her?' What does that mean?"

Agnus was manic. All the poise and professionalism she had possessed up to this point was draining out the back of her shifting eyes and expression. All that was left was a desperate, tired woman. Her lawyer lifted his hand and attempted to warn his client. Agnus, straining against the restraints swatted it away.

"I stopped her! I was willing to do whatever it took to keep my money from draining. If the world wasn't going to see her for how crazy she was, then I was going to make sure I showed them."

"Did you do that through her meds? The meds that Harold prescribed her?"

"We gave her the meds so that her true, insane self would be revealed."

"And your future son-in-law scared her into oblivion. At your command!"

"It's not my fault that she decided to jump from the balcony!"

Silence. There it was. The truth was revealed.

"Oh, but it is, Mrs. Palmitieri," explained the Detective. "You gave her a potentially lethal dose of Levodopa and set up a home invasion just to push her past her breaking point. Isn't that correct?"

"I showed the world who my mother was. A crazy woman who put too much stock in faith."

More silence. The realization struck Agnus like a fuel tanker. Her vision started spinning, and her eyes began to water. She had just confessed enough. The rest was history. No Russia. No millions. No new life or fresh start.

Next to her, her lawyer shook his head. All was revealed and on record. The truth prevailed.

Part 3: Where Does My Help Come From?

"For I know the plans I have for you, sayeth the Lord. Plans to

prosper you and not harm you..."

Numbers 32:23

Chapter 25

The fallout left behind by Agnus' arrest was nearly as clean and clinical as she had once been. As she was signing her confession in the interrogation room, the police were handcuffing Harold on the front lawn of their home. Some of the neighbors would later tell Arlene at church that they watched him cry. It was a sad sight. There was no fight or attempt to evade. When the cops arrived, Harold simply walked out and lifted his hands. It was like he was waiting on them all day.

The pre-trial hearing was set for a month after the arrest. Due to the nature of the crime, Harold, Michael, and Agnus were all detained until then. Bond was set for Harold and Agnus at $1 million, $5 million for Michael. Their assets were immediately seized so no one paid the bond. The pre-trial was over in 30 mins and the actual trial began a week after that.

All three were found guilty. Harold of accessory to murder, Agnus accessory to murder, and financial crimes towards an elder. Michael of 2nd-degree murder. Harold received 15 years, Agnus 25, and Michael 35.

For Georgianne, the grief behind her family's implosion was difficult. For obvious reasons, the wedding was called off. Thankfully, most of the financial purchases made by Georgianne and her parents, as well as a few items purchased by Michael's mother, were reimbursed. They hadn't purchased any food, thankfully, but just a week before everything fell apart, Georgianne had reserved the venue with her own money. Unfortunately, the deposit was nonrefundable, and Georgianne lost plenty.

Now, six months later, it was time for the family's first visit. Arlene had agreed to visit Agnus with Georgianne. When they were done there, they would run down to the men's penitentiary, which was only 15 miles away, to visit Michael and Harold. It was going to be a busy, emotional day.

Arlene gripped her cane tightly as she and Allison waited patiently in the living room. Allison leaned forward and brushed out the wrinkles in her skirt.

"You look beautiful, sweetheart," whispered Arlene.

"Thank you, mama," Allison answered. "I'm just nervous. More so for Georgianne. I just can't imagine what she's going through."

"I know," answered Arlene. "But that's why we are here. To help her through it."

At that, Georgianne appeared in the doorway. She wore a navy blue dress with a white belt around the waist. Her feet were clad with white sneakers, and about her neck was a gold necklace. Dangling at the end of it was a cross.

Arlene extended her arms out to Georgianne, who met her in her seat. "You look beautiful, Georgianne."

"Thank you, Aunt Arlene. You both ready?"

Allison drove the women towards the women's penitentiary on the outskirts of town. The visit was scheduled for noon. They arrived 20 minutes early as instructed for inspection and directions. They were each searched and wanded at the front gate and then again at the front door. After a few minutes of waiting in the lobby, they were escorted with a group of other visitors through a metal door and down a long corridor of bars and small windows. At the end of the hall, they exited out into a patio area with small tables scattered around. At one of the tables sat a small woman with blonde hair. The hair was haphazardly pulled back into a tight ponytail. The orange jumpsuit was brightly illuminated in the sun's rays.

Georgianne stopped at the door, nearly causing a crash of bodies behind her. Carefully, Allison grabbed her shoulders and helped her shift to the right, allowing the other visitors to pass. Arlene made her way behind them, slower than the rest, as her cane was confiscated at the gate.

"Georgianne, you don't have to do this," whispered Allison. "Not yet."

"No," she answered. "I want to. I just need a moment."

The three of them finally made it to the table where Agnus stood to greet them. Arlene saw Agnus' eyes dart to the ground when she looked at her. Immediately, Arlene silenced the mean thoughts that rose up. Now was not the time. This was a time for forgiveness.

"Hey Georgie," whispered Agnus. "I've missed you."

"Hey, Mom," Georgianne responded. "How are you holding up in here?"

The four of them found a seat around the table. "I'm doing as best as is expected. Mostly, the women keep to themselves. I just try to do the same."

No one said anything else for a moment. An awkward feeling began to bubble over.

"I recently started working in the library," continued Agnus. "It's nice. It's way better than outside work. I get to read whatever I want, which is great."

"That's nice," whispered Allison.

Another awkward moment. Agnus shifted in her chair once again. When no one said anything else, she cleared her throat.

"Listen, I don't know how to start this," she began. "I've thought a lot about what I was going to say when I saw you all. I know that what I did was wrong."

Arlene felt the hair on the back of her neck stand up. This was an attempt at an apology, which was a rare occurrence from her sister.

Agnus continued, "I'm so sorry for what I have done to this family. I never meant for this much harm. I honestly did not mean for mom to die."

"What did you mean to happen?" Georgianne responded quickly. Arlene could tell she was growing emotional. "You poisoned my grandmother. Your mother. What exactly did you expect to happen?"

"I just wanted you all to see what I had seen. She was making decisions that didn't make sense. Financially, she was...,"

"Agnus, don't," interrupted Arlene. "Don't go there. The last thing you should talk about right now is money. This was never about money. This was about control."

Silence again. Agnus lowered her head, defeated. Arlene was shocked. She had never seen her sister relent before.

"I just want to say I'm sorry. I'm sorry for everything."

Then she broke. Years of emotion, compartmentalized and hidden in the filing cabinets of her subconsciousness, came pouring out of her eyes and onto the concrete table. It was jarring. Her shoulders heaved, and a small moan hummed from deep in her lungs. Allison quickly looked back at Arlene, who met her gaze. Arlene felt her face flush and her cheeks burn red.

Then, like two songbirds in harmony, Georgianne broke with her. She instinctively grabbed her mother's hands and lowered her face into her arms. Both the women cried for what felt like 15 minutes, but it was only a couple. Wiping tears from their own eyes, Arlene and Allison waited respectfully.

When the tears began to subside, Arlene slowly lifted herself from her seat and made her way to her sister. Agnus leaned back, eyes bulging, not knowing what to expect. Her shoulders were stiff, and she braced herself for what she was certain would be a swift and justified retribution.

Arlene leaned in towards her sister, her shadow covering the now much skinnier frame of the convicted woman. Agnus closed her eyes and turned her head. Then, a second later, she snapped them open and realized the warmth of her sister's embrace. Arlene had leaned down and captured her sister in a hug of forgiveness. It was the first embrace the two sisters had shared since they were pre-teens. Agnus began crying hysterically as she leaned her head further into her sister, taking in the love and compassion.

"Why?" was all she was able to muster.

"Because," Arlene explained. "You are my sister. You are our mother's daughter. And you are a child of the Most High."

After ten more minutes, the women said their emotional farewells and "see you later" before Agnus was escorted along with the other inmates out of the courtyard first. She wasn't sure, but Arlene could almost sense that Agnus was walking lighter than before, as if she had lost a considerable amount of weight at that table.

Arlene and the two girls were escorted out the front door back to freedom. Immediately, they left the prison to head towards the men's penitentiary. There, they met with Harold for the first 15 minutes and Michael for the last 15.

Harold, a shell of his former imposing self, was contrite and apologetic. He had found a job serving in the nurse's station, given his medical background. All things considered, he was doing fine. His age and intelligence served him well in prison, and the others left him alone.

Michael, on the other hand, was not doing well at all. Due to the nature of his crime, he was often the subject of many other inmates' wrath. Inmates didn't take kindly to those who "preyed" on the weak. In their eyes, Michael murdered their own grandmothers and mothers. Despite Michael's plea for understanding, this often means fights and attacks. Georgianne's heart broke when she saw him behind the plated glass. His face was bruised, and he had lost a considerable amount of weight.

In prison, both Harold and Michael found Christ. Michael leaned on his strong foundation from his teenage years and consulted with the prison chaplain regularly, eventually rededicating his life to Christ during the second Sunday service after he arrived. Harold, on the other hand, considered the decision for the first few months. But, after talking with his cellmate, a reformed believer with a terrible past, he gave his heart to Christ in his cell—no crowd or pastor. Just two sinners saved by Grace.

Allison and Arlene didn't return to the prison except for a couple of times per year. Georgianne, however, found herself back at her mother's side nearly 2-3 times per month. Their bond grew stronger as Agnus quickly learned to listen rather than control. Oddly enough, with prison walls between them, the mother and daughter grew closer than ever before.

The only thing: Agnus refused to discuss faith. Georgianne wasn't entirely sure why. It seemed as if Agnus, though claiming not to believe in God, essentially blamed God for where she had ended up. Georgianne didn't pry, and when the subject came up about her pursuing ministry and seminary, she would respectfully avoid discussing faith and personal beliefs. Regardless, Agnus seemed intrigued with her daughter's new path.

Nearly completing her undergraduate degree in pastoral leadership with an emphasis on missions, Georgianne had big plans to start her own ministry. The only drawback was that all the money that her parents had made in their schemes was split between court costs and attorney fees, with the rest confiscated by the government. This essentially meant Georgianne was inadvertently written out of her grandparents' will with no claim to the estate. She worked as a barista in the evenings at the local coffee shop, where she made just enough to pay for what her student loan didn't cover and the small apartment she moved into once her parents' home was foreclosed.

"Do you think your Aunt Arlene would help?" asked Agnus at one point. "At least just to start the LLC?"

"I don't want to ask her," Georgianne responded. "It just doesn't seem right to get anything after everything that happened."

She could tell the words stung her mother despite their truth. To help salve the wounds, she added, "But I know God has a plan for me."

Agnus didn't respond. She just smiled and hugged her daughter again.

Chapter 26

It was the first Christmas since the trial and only the second after Phyllis had passed. Needless to say, the whole family was emotional.

For Georgianne, this was doubly so. Allison had organized a family get-together on Christmas Eve for all members of Phyllis' family. Six months earlier, she had been completely wrapped in her new groundbreaking event for her new building. Her event scheduling company had grown quickly and was expanding across the state. Now that the busyness was settled for a while, she wanted to do something special for the family. The goal was to bring everyone together under one roof and "only focus on the good things," as Allison had described it in the invitation. To Arlene's surprise, both her brothers and their families agreed to come. Arlene's brothers had started to interact more than usual, especially given the fact that Arlene was able to fulfill her mother's final wishes. Both men and their families received a substantial part of the estate once the government took their share, with the remainder split evenly between the three siblings. Arlene made sure to take care of herself as she promised and then, in turn, blessed her family.

The main event was to be hosted at Arlene's new home—the house her family had grown up in. Just three months earlier, the owners who had purchased it from Agnus put it up on the market due to a job transfer. Arlene was able, thanks to the money left over from her medical bills and Allison's schooling, to offer above the asking price. She moved in a month before Christmas.

Her surgery, paid for by Phyllis, had been a success, and she had started to gain back a considerable amount of her mobility. Though she was still using a cane, she walked freely between the rooms and spent most of her time in the kitchen while Allison, Georgianne, and she all finalized the preparations for the get-together that evening. Sounds of laughter and kids playing were heard in the living room as Arlene's brothers and their wives and children reminisced about childhood and the time they spent coming and going from home.

That evening, the dinner was picked clean, and small gifts were swapped around a large Christmas tree. There were smiles and laughter and the occasional tears as memories of Phyllis filled the air. It was a beautiful time, just as Allison had designed it to be. Around 10 in the evening, Arlene's oldest brother said his goodbyes, and the final family members left the house, leaving behind Arlene, Georgianne, and Allison.

Georgianne threw away the last garbage back in the can out back and returned to the kitchen, where Allison and Arlene sat at the table, snickering like schoolgirls.

"Uh oh," said Georgianne with a smile. "What are you two up to know?"

"Georgianne, come sit with us," Arlene said with her coffee in hand. "We want to talk to you about something."

Georgianne grabbed her coffee cup and sat next to Allison, opposite her Aunt, who continued to smile wide.

"What's going on?"

"Allison, do you want to do the honors?" asked Arlene.

Allison nodded and turned towards her cousin, smiling from ear to ear.

"Georgie, we know that these past few months have been really hard on you. And we want you to know that we are here for you."

"Oh, I know that," responded Georgianne quickly. "You two have always been there for me."

"Well, we want you to let us be there for you one more time," Allison continued.

Arlene placed her coffee down on the table and reached for her pocketbook.

"Before your grandmother passed, she would often tell me how proud she was of the strong, Christian woman you were becoming. She loved your heart for missions."

Georgianne felt tears stinging her eyes. Arlene pulled out an envelope from her pocketbook. Around it was a red ribbon tied in a bow. In bold, beautiful letters was written: To Georgianne.

"Once you started going to church, your grandmother would always tell me how she dreamt of one day being a small part of your future ministry."

Arlene handed the envelope to Georgianne, who wiped the tears from her eyes. Carefully, she slid the ribbon off and opened it up. Inside was a folded piece of printer paper. She looked up at her aunt and cousin, who both nodded and smiled. With great care, she pulled out the envelope and unfolded it. In large, bold letters, it read.

The certificate hereby awards Georgianne Palmitieri with a 501(c)3 status under the name:

World Outreach Missions, Inc.

At the bottom of the certificate, which granted the validity of Georgianne's ministry status and confirmed the title she had always wanted in the country's registry, was a paperclipped check. The amount read: $150,000.

Georgianne broke. Tears gushed down her cheeks. Through smeared vision, she searched for her aunt's face. When she found it, she saw tears falling down Arlene's cheeks as well.

"Georgianne," Arlene reassured. "God has never been caught off guard through any of this. He's known the plans He's had for you since the beginning."

Georgianne nodded between sobs while Allison, crying as well, rubbed her back with her hand.

Arlene continued, "Your grandparents loved you and wanted so badly for you to find your purpose and pursue your dreams. And now, they can?. Because of all the hard work and prayer you've put into this, they can?. That money is for you to begin. However, you need to. We love you."

The women embraced each other and cried tears and relief and joy as small snowflakes drifted in front of the window in the kitchen. Soft Christmas music drifted in from the living room radio.

Between sniffles and cries and a few hearty laughs, the words of a familiar song were heard:

...the Savior reigns.

Let all the songs employ.

While fields and floods, rocks, hills, and plains

Repeat the sound of joy...

THE END